ALSO BY GORDON KORMAN

Born to Rock
Son of the Mob
Son of the Mob 2: Hollywood Hustle
Jake, Reinvented
Maxx Comedy
The 6th Grade Nickname Game
Son of Interflux
I Want to Go Home
No Coins, Please
Radio Fifth Grade

Series:
Kidnapped
On the Run
Island
Dive
Everest
Macdonald Hall

SCHOOLED

Gordon Korman

SCHOLASTIC CANADA LTD.
Toronto New York London Auckland Sydney
Mexico City New Delhi Hong Kong Buenos Aires

For my Aunt Shirley

Scholastic Canada Ltd.
604 King Street West, Toronto, Ontario M5V 1E1, Canada

Scholastic Inc.
557 Broadway, New York, NY 10012, USA

Scholastic Australia Pty Limited
PO Box 579, Gosford, NSW 2250, Australia

Scholastic New Zealand Limited
Private Bag 94407, Greenmount, Auckland, New Zealand

Scholastic Children's Books
Euston House, 24 Eversholt Street, London NW1 1DB, UK

Library and Archives Canada Cataloguing in Publication
Korman, Gordon
    Schooled / Gordon Korman.

ISBN 978-0-545-99990-8 (bound).--ISBN 978-0-545-99458-3
(paper over board).--ISBN 978-0-545-99321-0 (pbk.)
    I. Title.

PS8571.O78S36 2007   jC813'.54   C2007-901041-5
PS8571*

ISBN-10 0-545-99321-0
This book is set in 12-point Janson Text.
Designed by Ellice Lee.

Cover photographs, front to back:
© Royalty-Free/Hemera Technologies/Jupiter Images;
© Royalty-Free/Comstock Images/Jupiter Images.

6 5 4 3 2 1   Printed in Canada   08 09 10 11 12 13

1

NAME: **CAPRICORN ANDERSON**

I was thirteen the first time I saw a police officer up close. He was arresting me for driving without a license. At the time, I didn't even know what a license was. I wasn't too clear on what being arrested meant either.

But by then they were loading Rain onto a stretcher to rush her in for X-rays. So I barely noticed the handcuffs the officer slapped on my wrists.

"Who's the owner of this pickup?"

"It belongs to the community," I told him.

He made a note on a ring-bound pad. "What community? Golf club? Condo deal?"

"Garland Farm."

He frowned. "Never heard of that one."

Rain would have been pleased. That was the whole point of the community—to allow us to escape the money-hungry rat race of modern society. If people didn't know us, they couldn't find us, and we could live our lives in peace.

"It's an alternative farm commune," I explained.

The officer goggled at me. "Alternative—you mean like *hippies*?"

"Rain used to be one, back in the sixties. There were fourteen families at Garland then. Now it's just Rain and me." I tried to edge my way toward the nursing station. "I have to make sure she's okay."

He was unmoved. "Who is this Rain? According to her Social Security card, the patient's name is Rachel Esther Rosenblatt."

"Her name is Rain, and she's my grandmother," I said stiffly. "She fell out of a tree."

He stared at his notes. "What was a sixty-seven-year-old woman doing up a tree?"

"Picking plums," I replied defensively. "She slipped."

"So you drove her here. At thirteen."

"I drive all the time," I informed him. "Rain

taught me when I was eight."

Sweat appeared on his upper lip. "And you never thought of just dialing 911?"

I regarded him blankly. "What's nine-one-one?"

"The emergency number! On the telephone!"

I told him the truth. "I've talked on a telephone a couple of times. In town. But we don't have one."

He looked at me for what seemed like forever. "What's your name, son?"

"Cap. It's short for Capricorn."

He unlocked my handcuffs. I was un-arrested.

How could an able-bodied teenager allow his grand-mother to scale a plum tree? Simple. She wasn't my grandmother at the time. She was my teacher.

I was homeschooled. That was the law. Even on a tiny farm like ours, you had to get an education. No school bus could ever make it up the rutted, snaking dirt road that led to Garland. But transportation wasn't the only problem. If we'd been serviced by an eight-lane highway, Rain still would have handled my schooling personally. We wanted to avoid the low standards and cultural poison of a world that had lost its way.

So that's what I was doing when Rain fell—working on a vocabulary lesson. Most of the list came from the state eighth grade curriculum: *barometer, decagon, perpendicular* . . .

I could always spot the extra words Rain threw in: *nonviolence, Zen Buddhism, psychedelic* . . .

Microprocessor? I frowned at the paper on the unpainted wooden table. Was that Rain or the state? I'd never heard that term before.

I stepped out of the house, careful not to disturb my science project—the Foucault pendulum suspended from the porch roof. The tester from the education department thought it was good enough to enter in the county science fair. Too bad we didn't believe in competition—all that emphasis on trophies and medals, the shiny symbols of an empty soul. Anyway, Rain said the whole thing was a trick to get me to go to regular school.

"If your project is excellent, it only proves that you're getting a superior education right here with me" had been her reasoning.

I spotted her up in the tree, reaching across a limb to pick a plum. "Rain," I called, "there's a word I don't under—"

And it happened. One minute she was on the

branch; the next she was on the ground. I don't even recall seeing her fall. Just the faint cry followed by the dull clunk.

"Aaah!" *Whump.*

"Rain!"

She was lying on her side amid the scattered plums when I pounded onto the scene. Her face was very pale. She wasn't moving.

My terror was total. Rain was everything to me—my teacher, my family, my whole universe. Garland was a community, but *we* were the community—the two of us!

I knelt beside her. "Rain—are you okay? Please be okay!"

Her eyes fluttered open and focused on me. She tried to smile, but the pain contorted her expression into a grimace. "Cap—" she began faintly.

I leaped back to my feet. "I'll get Doc Cafferty!"

Doc Cafferty lived a few miles away. He was technically a veterinarian. But he was used to working on humans, since he had six kids. He'd given me stitches once when I was eight.

She reached up a tremulous hand and gripped my arm. "We need a real doctor this time. A people doctor."

I stared at her like she was speaking a foreign language. Doc Cafferty had filled all of Garland's medical needs as long as I could remember.

She spelled it out. "You're going to have to take me to the hospital."

Rain always said that anger upsets the balance inside a person. So when you yell at somebody, you're attacking yourself more than whoever it is you're yelling at.

Falling out of the tree must have made her forget this. Because when the nurses finally let me in to see her, she was screaming at the doctor at top volume. *"I can't do eight weeks of rehab! I can't do eight days!"*

"You've got no choice," the doctor said matter-of-factly. "You have a broken hip. It has to be pinned. After that you'll need extensive physical therapy. It's a long process, and you can't ignore it just because it doesn't fit in with your plans."

"You're not listening!" Rain shrilled. "I'm the caregiver to my grandson! The *only* caregiver!"

"What about the parents?" the doctor asked. "Where are they?"

She shook her head. "Long dead. Malaria. They

were with the Peace Corps in Namibia. They gave their lives for what they believed in."

That sounds worse than it is. But I never knew my parents except from old pictures. They left when I was little. Besides, the rule at Garland back then was that we all belonged to each other, and it didn't matter who was related by blood. I have a few vague recollections of other people in the community when I was really young. But whether they were my parents or not, I can't tell. Anyway, it's impossible to miss what you never had.

I rushed to my grandmother's bedside. "Are you okay? Is your leg all fixed up?"

She looked grave. "We've got a problem, Cap. And you know what we do with problems."

"We talk it out, think it out, work it out," I said readily. It had been that way since the very beginning of Garland in 1967, long before I was born. Now that there were only two of us, Rain still gave me a full vote. She never treated me like I was just a kid.

The doctor was growing impatient. "How about cousins? Or maybe a close friend from school?"

"I'm homeschooled," I supplied.

The doctor sighed. "Mrs. Rosenblatt—"

"That name hasn't applied to me for decades. You can call me Rain."

"All right. Rain. I'm admitting you now. We'll operate in the morning. And I'll call social services to see what arrangements can be made for your grandson."

That was when I started to worry about what was going to happen to me.

2

NAME: **MRS. DONNELLY**

The instant I saw him standing there with all that hair and all those beads, I just knew.

Garland Farm. It had to be. Nobody else looked like that. Nobody *had* looked like that since 1970. Except at Garland.

He seemed terrified, and with good reason. No one knew what lay ahead for him better than I did.

I held out my hand. "I'm Mrs. Donnelly."

He made no move to take it. "Capricorn."

Capricorn. Wasn't that just classic? My own name, Flora, was short for Floramundi—a world of flowers.

I'd been out of that place more than thirty years,

but one sight of this kid, and it all came roaring back in a tsunami of Day-Glo ponchos and organic lentils.

I was five when my family joined the community—too young to remember any life before that. For six long years, that place was my universe. I ran around barefoot, wearing peasant dresses, shared my parents with the other kids, protested the Vietnam War, did farm chores, and listened to a whole lot of sitar music.

So help me, I didn't know how weird it all was until my parents decided they were too old to be hippies anymore, and we rejoined the real world. That part I remember like it was yesterday—this little flower child, who barely knew how a doorknob worked, suddenly dropped in the middle of a society several centuries ahead of the one she'd just left.

I looked at Capricorn Anderson, and that's what I saw—not a case, but a time traveler, about to step into a world that had forgotten the sixties except for J.F.K. and the Beatles.

In my right hand was a piece of paper with the address of the foster home the Department of Child Services had assigned for this boy. I crumpled it up and tossed it into the nearest trash can.

"Well, Capricorn, it looks like you're going to be staying at my house for a few weeks."

"Absolutely not!" he exclaimed. "I have to get back to the community. The plums aren't in yet. And after that the apples. Everything has to be ready for when Rain comes home."

I remembered Rain. She was one of the founders of Garland, the queen bee of the place when I lived there. I was always afraid of her. I thought she was a witch.

"Wait a minute—" I put two and two together. "Rachel Esther Rosenblatt is *Rain*? Your grand-mother?"

He brightened. "You know her?"

That's when I figured out the key to Capricorn's heart, so I could do what needed to be done for his own good.

"I used to. Way back before you were born, my family lived at Garland. Rain would want you to be with someone who understands."

I had a reluctant houseguest.

3

NAME: **ZACH POWERS**

I high-fived my way off the school bus, slapping hands on both sides of the aisle.

"Hey, Zach!"

"How's it going, man?"

I jumped down to the tarmac of the school's driveway. It was a beautiful September day. This was my time—eighth grade, captain of the football and soccer teams, Big Man on Campus. After two years of looking up to other people, I'd finally made it to the point where there was nobody to look up to but me.

Everything was perfect.

I frowned. Well, not quite perfect. I noticed that

the sign on the front lawn read:

WELCOME TO CLAVERAGE MIDDLE SCHOOL

They'd fixed it again. Unacceptable.

I did a quick scan to confirm there were no teachers looking on. Mr. Sorenson's eyes were on the buses, so his back was turned. I reached up and snatched off a letter. The sign now read:

WELCOME TO C AVERAGE MIDDLE SCHOOL

Much better. I stuffed the *L* behind the bushes and walked on, enjoying the admiration of some seventh grade girls. It was a dangerous job, but somebody had to do it. At C Average Middle School, the buck stopped with me.

Not that I was nobody last year. I was still probably the most happening seventh grader in the place. But it isn't really your school until you're a senior. I wasn't going to drop the ball on any of it.

For example, the election for eighth grade president was coming up. Not that I was running myself. God forbid. The tradition at C Average was to nominate the biggest loser in the building. No one runs against him, of course, and he wins auto-matically. Then, for the rest of the year, you get the pleasure of watching President Bonehead giving speeches, running assemblies, and making a complete idiot out of himself.

It's top-notch entertainment—*if* you nail exactly the right guy.

I was pretty sure I had the front-runner all picked out. Ever since kindergarten, the primo nerd, bar none, had been Hugh Winkleman. Over the years, the doofus had been on the receiving end of so many wedgies that he had elastic waistband material fused to the top of his head—pardon the exaggeration.

In a million years, there could not have been any-one more perfect for this job than Hugh. Or so I thought.

I was on my way to homeroom when Mr. Kasigi, the assistant principal, flagged me down. Standing beside him was the strangest-looking kid I'd ever seen. He was tall and skinny as a rake. I swear he'd never been anywhere near a barbershop in his life. His long blond flyaway hair stretched all the way down to the middle of his back. His clothes looked like pajamas—*homemade* pajamas. And his shoes were something out of a social studies project on the pioneer days. They were sandals woven out of cornhusks, and rustled when he moved.

Kasigi introduced us. "Zachary Powers, meet Capricorn Anderson. Cap just transferred here."

Yeah, from the planet Krypton.

"Show him to locker 743 and make sure he gets to homeroom." He rushed off in the direction of the office.

The weirdest thing about Capricorn Anderson was this: *he* was looking at *me* like *I* was the freak. Like he'd never seen another kid before!

"Come on, Cap. Follow me."

We walked down the hall, picking up more than our fair share of attention.

"New kid," I said aloud, just in case anybody thought he was actually *with* me. "Kasigi asked me to show him around."

Locker 743. "Here it is," I told him. "You've got the combo, right?"

He just stared at me blankly.

"The combination," I prompted. "There— printed on top of your orientation form."

"But what does it mean?"

I would have sworn he was putting me on, except he looked so bewildered.

17

"Here—I'll show you. Seventeen . . . thirty-three . . . five." There was a click, and the door swung wide.

He peered in as if he expected to find a mountain lion lying in wait. "It's empty."

He was beginning to rile me. "Of course it's empty. It's *your* locker. It's empty until you put something in it."

"What do *I* have to put in there?" he demanded.

"How should I know? It's *your* stuff."

"When we lock things away," he said with conviction, "we're really imprisoning ourselves."

Now, that was definitely something you didn't hear every day. "What school did you go to before this?"

"I'm homeschooled," he informed me. "I'm only here because Rain broke her hip, and they won't let me live alone at the community."

Hugh Winkleman, you're a lucky man. With the arrival of this new kid, all the losers in school were bumped down one space. Never before had anyone screamed for the job of eighth grade president like Capricorn Anderson.

This was my year!

4

NAME: **CAPRICORN ANDERSON**

"What are you looking at, jerkface?"

"What are *you* looking at, buttwipe?"

The first boy swung his book bag around and slammed it into the side of the other's head. *He* responded by punching the first boy in the nose, and soon the two were rolling on the grass, grunting and raining blows on one another.

I was horrified. I'd read about physical violence, but this was the first time I'd witnessed it in real life. It was sudden and lightning fast. Wild, vicious, ugly.

In seconds, a ring of spectators formed around the brawlers. Their gleeful chant echoed all around the schoolyard.

"Fight! Fight! Fight! Fight! . . ."

"Break it up!" A teacher burst into the circle, a brawny man with a whistle around his neck. He squeezed himself between the combatants and pushed them apart. "All right, who started it?"

"He did!" the two chorused, each pointing at his opponent.

The teacher gazed around at the spectators. "Any witnesses?" Nobody said a word. "Come on, who saw what happened?"

"I did," I volunteered.

"Well?"

"Buttwipe wanted to know what jerkface was looking at, and jerkface wanted to know what butt-wipe was looking at." I turned earnest eyes on the bloody and dirt-smeared brawlers. "You were barely three inches apart. Couldn't you see you were both looking at each other?"

The teacher reddened. "Who do you think you are, Jerry Seinfeld?"

"You must have me confused with another student," I told him. "My name is Capricorn Anderson."

"Are you talking back to me?"

I hesitated. The whistle-teacher had asked me a

question, and I'd answered by talking. "Yes?" I ventured uncertainly.

By the time he was finished yelling, both fighters had boarded their buses and gone home. *I* was the one who got sent to Mr. Kasigi's office.

I was waiting on the bench when Mrs. Donnelly appeared.

I leaped up. "Is Rain going to be okay?"

"That's why I'm here. Let's take a ride over there and find out." Her brow furrowed. "What are you doing in the hot seat?"

"I have a smart mouth," I replied honestly. "It's against the rules."

She began leading me down the hall. "Come on, we've got a long drive. I'll straighten everything out with Mr. Kasigi."

It took more than an hour to get to the hospital, but it was worth it. Good news—Rain's operation was a success.

"So we can go back home?" I asked anxiously.

Rain smiled sadly. "The doctor was right. This is going to be a long recovery. And because it's only the two of us at Garland, they're not going to release me early." She held my hand. "I know you're upset, but we're just going to have to be strong."

"I don't like it out there," I complained. "It's too crowded. People dress funny; they talk too fast; and all they're interested in is *things*! Cell phones and iPods and Game Boys and Starbucks. What's a starbuck?"

She looked upset, and older than I'd ever seen her before. "I want you to listen to me, Cap, and try not to blame me."

"Blame you?"

"I believe in the community," she began, "and I believe in the life we've built together. But I was fooling myself to think that you were still so young that you wouldn't have to learn about the world outside ours. It's not a nice place, and I didn't want you tossed into it without a little more preparation."

I'd read about depression, but this was the first time I'd actually felt it. It was like a stone pressing down on my chest. I couldn't lift it off because I didn't have the strength.

"I'm kind of scared, Rain."

"Well, don't be," she said firmly. "All you have to do is focus on who you are and what your values mean to you. You've passed every state test—always in the top five percent. You're as smart and capable as anybody—more than most."

"What I saw in school today wasn't on any test," I observed grimly.

She gave me a sympathetic smile. "True, information isn't the same as experience. You know what television is, but you've never watched it. You know what pizza is, but you've never tasted any. You know about friendships, but you've never had a friend."

"*You're* my friend."

"Of course I am," she agreed. "But I'm not exactly a teenager."

"I'm already finished with other teenagers. I've been in real school for one day, and that's plenty. People are constantly screaming at each other. Two boys actually resorted to physical violence! I thought violence only happened in crimes and wars, but this was over—" I shrugged helplessly. "I can't even explain it."

"You have to feel sorry for them," Rain said with a sigh. "Nonviolence isn't something everyone understands."

"They've got these things called lockers," I raved on. "The halls are lined with them. And you won't believe what they're for! They're for locking stuff away—so other people won't steal it! Why can't everybody just share?"

Rain must have agreed with me, because she looked really worried.

I poured it on thick. "They don't have regular time at school, you know. They have *periods*. All of a sudden an alarm goes off and you're supposed to drop what you're doing and rush off to a different room with a different teacher to do something completely different! How can anybody learn like that?"

There was a knock at the door, and Mrs. Donnelly poked her head into the room. She lived at Garland for a while when she was a kid, so she understood how great it was and how much I wanted to get back there.

"Hello, Rain. How are you feeling?"

"It's been a long time, Floramundi." Rain looked her up and down. "It's wonderful to see that you've done well since your family abandoned the lifestyle and value system they believed in."

They talked about her parents and a few other people. Some of the names were familiar, but I didn't remember anybody. The days of Garland as a thriving commune were over long before I was born in 1994.

It was a friendly conversation, but every time Rain called her Floramundi, Mrs. Donnelly got kind of tense. Maybe that was because her family left Garland, so she couldn't live there anymore. I knew how that felt.

Anyway, we were soon on our way home—her home, not mine, unfortunately.

Her house was pretty nice, except it had too many stairs. There didn't seem to be any more purpose for them than there had been for the fight at school earlier in the day. The living room was a few steps down; the bedrooms were a few steps up; and the kitchen was in the middle. Mrs. Donnelly called it a split-level. But what was the point of splitting a house when you could just make it flat and not have any stairs at all?

Everything was more complicated in the world outside the community. The buildings at Garland were made of wood, period. Here there was wood in some places, but also brick, stone, and aluminum. Inside, there was carpet and tile, white walls and other colors, and hundreds of pictures, curtains, tassels, clocks, figurines, and a million different things that might have been useful, but might have been just for decoration too. Who could tell? It seemed like an awful lot of stuff for just one house.

Mrs. Donnelly lived here with her daughter, Sophie. And, of course, me, now.

Sophie was sixteen. She went to the high school. *I* didn't much like it that I had to be here. Multiply that by fifty, and that's how much Sophie didn't like it that I had to be here.

"Mother—are you on drugs? How could you bring that—that *freakazoid* into our house?"

"Shhh—Sophie. He'll hear you."

"I want him to hear me!" Sophie shrieked. "How else is he going to get the message to clear out?"

"He has nowhere else to go," Mrs. Donnelly pleaded.

"And that's *my* problem? Just because he comes from the same hippie-dippie flea circus where you grew up doesn't mean we have to adopt him!"

"Lower your voice," her mother ordered sternly. "It's only for six weeks—two months at the outside."

"Two *months*? I have to live my life! Do you know how long it took me to get Josh Weintraub to ask me out? What's he going to think when he

26

drives up and sees this tie-dyed streak of misery draped across the porch?"

This whole conversation went on before either of us had spoken a single word to the other. I didn't actually talk to Sophie until later that night when I accidentally blundered into her room. She was in her pajamas, speaking on the phone while smearing pale green cream all over her face.

She threw down the handset. "You. Out. *Now*."

I stood frozen, staring at her. "What—what's on your face?"

"Oh, right, you've never heard of moisturizer. You were just looking for an excuse to come busting into my room!"

I was mystified. "What are you moisturizing?"

She stamped a slippered foot. "My skin, genius! It's a beauty product, okay? Scram!"

I backed out into the hallway. She slammed the door with such force I'm amazed the wall didn't crumble. The one at Garland probably would have.

There I stood, still facing her door, paralyzed with discovery. Beauty. That was precisely the word that had been haunting me. Sophie Donnelly was beautiful. I had seen beautiful girls on book jackets, and even noticed some from a distance when Rain and I had gone into town for supplies. But this was the first time I'd ever really met one. I never could have imagined how strong the effect would be. Just standing near her—even when she was yelling at me—made me feel . . . nice.

It sure was a strange and complex world outside Garland.

5

NAME: **HUGH WINKLEMAN**

Adults are always trying to figure out what makes kids tick. They send professors into middle schools to do research and run tests; they publish thousand-page studies.

Know what? They don't have a clue.

If you want to understand middle school students, there's only one way to do it: follow the wedgies. Wedgie-givers and wedgie-receivers. Take it from someone who's been down that road before.

Sad to say, I'm one of the receivers. Zach Powers, Lena Young, and their crowd ride rough-shod over a lot of people. But if statistics were taken, I'd be victim number one.

Until Capricorn Anderson showed up.

Even *I* could pick on a guy like that. Not that I'd ever do such a thing. I'd never lower myself to the level of those nitwits. But what a kid.

He wasn't nerdy in a typical way. He wasn't a computer geek or captain of the chess club (that was me). He couldn't speak Klingon; in fact, he'd never even heard of *Star Trek*. But just one peek at the guy and you knew that, dweebwise, there was a new sheriff in town.

A lot of eyes were on him as he sat down in the cafeteria. God, it felt good to have them staring at someone else for a change. I walked over to him. A guy like this was going to need all the friends he could get (one).

"Capricorn, right?" I set my tray down across from him. "I'm Hugh—from social studies class." I stuck my hand out, but he just stared at it. It wasn't a snub. Believe me, I could teach a college course on snubs. This was cluelessness. He honestly didn't know what to do.

"I remember you," he said finally. "There are so many people here. It's hard to keep track."

"I can help you with that." I pointed to the table where Zach and Lena were holding court. "That crowd thinks they own the place. They think that because they do. Stay away from them. They'll chop you up and press you into salami. Now, anyone you see hanging around their crew falls into one of two subgroups—the jocks and the wannabes. Stay away from both. And you definitely don't want anything to do with goths, burnouts, skateboarders, hip-hop kids, environmentalists, or anybody who has a baseball cap on backward." I took note of the blank expression on his face. "You know, standard survival skills. I'm sure it was similar at your old school."

"I was homeschooled before this."

"No kidding." I'd heard of that, but I'd never met anybody who did it. "What's it like?"

"Wonderful," he said wanly.

"I'll bet!" My enthusiasm was genuine. "It must be nice to wake up in the morning and not have to worry about walking into a hostile environment, with your next wedgie a matter of not *if* but *when*."

"What's a wedgie?"

Wow. Homeschooling must be heaven! I didn't answer the question. He'd find out soon enough.

My eyes fell on Cap's lunch, which consisted of salad, carrot sticks, and two slices of whole wheat bread. He must have noticed, because he was look-ing just as cur-iously at my hamburger.

"What part of the animal does that meat come from?"

"I don't know." I chewed thoughtfully. "The lips, probably. Want a bite?"

"I'm a vegetarian."

At that moment, I heard an all-too-familiar *thpoot* coming from behind us. Maybe one kid in a thousand would have recognized the sound. But I'm that kid. It was an incoming spitball.

I tensed, waiting for impact. But it wasn't aimed at me. Instead, I watched the tiny projectile land and lodge itself amid Cap's cascading piles of long hair. He didn't even feel it. Hermits could hole up in all that hair, and no two would ever meet.

At Zach's table, a celebration was going on, with lots of backslapping and high fives. Darryl Penny-field, Zach's football buddy and co-Neanderthal, was horsing around. Deadeye, I called him, but never to his face. When his face was too close, mine was usually being stuffed into a locker. Then I caught sight of the straw in Naomi Erlanger's hand. I guess Cap's mop was an irresistible target for ama-teur spitballers, not just the professionals.

The PA system came to life with the voice of Mr. Kasigi. "Just a reminder—the election for eighth grade president will be held on Tuesday, September twenty-sixth. The position is open to all eighth graders. So far, only one name has been placed in nomination—Capricorn Anderson. Thank you."

I was blown away. "You're running for president? In your first week here?"

Cap scanned the ceiling. "Who *is* that? If he wants to talk to us, why doesn't he just come into the room?"

"But why is he talking about *you*?" I persisted. "*Are* you running for president?"

"Of course not. I don't believe in government. I come from an autonomous collective."

"But Mr. Kasigi said—" And suddenly, I just knew.

The triumphant grins on the smug faces of Zach and company told the whole story. Cap hadn't placed his name in nomination. Zach had done it for him. I'd heard something about this last year. The eighth graders had picked this computer genius, Luke Simard, and got him elected president just so they could make fun of him. By the end of the year, the poor kid was so crazy that he skipped graduation and applied to an alternative high school so he wouldn't have to face four more years with the people who'd made his life so miserable.

Now we were the eighth graders, and it was our turn to do the same thing. Only, instead of picking the smartest guy in school, Zach had zeroed in on somebody who didn't even seem to know what a PA system was.

I opened my mouth to issue the warning. The words were forming on my tongue: *Cap—get over to the office this minute and take yourself out of nomination! Do it now, before it's too late—*

And then it hit me. If Cap Anderson had never been born, the name announced to the whole school would have been mine. My strange and hairy new friend was the only thing preventing me from being the next Luke Simard.

I shut my mouth and kept it shut, trying to keep my eyes off the spitball still lodged just above Cap's left ear. I felt bad about it, but I felt something else too:

Better him than me.

6

NAME: **NAOMI ERLANGER**

The time was coming. I could almost smell it.

One day Zach Powers was going to be my boyfriend. Sure, he was sniffing around Lena—everybody knew that. But sooner or later he'd see that she lacked the depth and sincerity of yours truly, and that, besides, she had the hots for Darryl, or maybe Grant Tubman, if only he'd get rid of that ridiculous tongue stud that looked like a pimple. Enough said—especially about Lena, who was my best friend.

It was tough to compete with Lena, who was so naturally pretty and had a very strong personality. To be honest, she was kind of a bulldozer when it came to getting what she wanted, but I don't say that in a mean way. People did what she told them to because they liked her—not just because she'd make their lives miserable if they didn't. And since I was more shy than Lena, and not quite so willing to squeeze into size-zero jeans and apply makeup with a snow blower, I had to try a little harder to get Zach's attention.

Who would have thought that the equalizer would turn out to be the biggest dweeb in school? No, not Hugh Winkleman. Capricorn Anderson.

The minute I shot that spitball in the cafeteria, I could feel Zach noticing me. He said, "Nice trajectory," and he asked if he could finish my Tater Tots. I knew it was the turning point in our relationship. The road to Zach went straight through the new hippie kid.

Example: Zach wanted to make Cap eighth grade president. Sure, the rest of us had our hearts set on Winkleman, but I quickly volunteered to work on Cap's election campaign. Not that anybody was running against him, but we still had to make it look real so Mr. Kasigi wouldn't get suspicious.

We made posters. My favorite was: CAPRICORN ANDERSON—THE PEOPLE'S CHOICE, because while I was painting it, Zach said, "It doesn't have to be perfect, Naomi. It's not like anybody's going to have to vote for him." And while he was talking, his hand brushed my hand.

Lena was a little suspicious when I told her we didn't need any help with the election. You definitely didn't want to get on her bad side. But by the time Zach and I started going out, she'd probably be hot and heavy with Darryl (or Grant Tubman, minus the tongue stud). So I was safe.

Zach was so cool. It was almost like watching the plan beamed straight from his brain onto the screen of a blockbuster movie. We put up the posters, scared off two dummies who wanted to run for the job, and presto! Capricorn Anderson was elected eighth grade president, unopposed.

"The best part is the doofus has no idea what just happened to him," Zach chortled.

"Who knows what's going on under all that hair?" snorted Lena.

I personally got the impression that Cap thought all new students had to go through this. Like being president was part of registering and choosing electives. But I kept my mouth shut and laughed along with the others. Zach had a great smile.

When they made the announcement at the all-school assembly, Zach and Darryl hoisted the new president up on their shoulders and marched him onto the stage. He'd been around C Average for a couple of weeks, and people knew his name from our posters and had seen him in the halls. But this was the first time the entire student body made the connection. Eleven hundred kids took in the sight of a genuine middle school hippie—this tall, skinny, longhaired boy in tie-dye, toes poking out of those homemade sandals. He looked so silly, so goofy, so *weird* that he was almost cute. Not attractive, but adorable in the sense that you can't help pitying him—like a wet puppy rolled in sand.

Zach started shouting, "Speech! Speech!" and some other people took up the cry.

Mr. Kasigi handed over the microphone, and we all quieted down to listen to what Cap had to say.

He stared at us for a long time, until I was almost wondering if Zach had chosen someone who was so nerdy he was *too* perfect for the job.

Then he announced, "I shouldn't be president."

"*Why not?*" Darryl heckled.

Cap struggled with that one. But when he finally spoke, his answer was as bizarre as his appearance: "I—I don't know anybody's name."

Like the president had to be able to rattle off the names of all eleven hundred of his constituents or else he wasn't qualified. Peals of laughter rolled through the gym. Even the sixth graders could see how dopey that was.

I felt proud and exhilarated. I felt like the woman that's behind every great man—the one behind Zach, I mean. "That was fantastic!" I congratulated him when the assembly was over.

He grabbed me by the arm and began towing me to the front. "We're not done yet."

"Where are we going?"

His oh-so-blue eyes gleamed. "If the hairball thinks it's his duty to learn eleven hundred names, who are we to burst his bubble by telling him he doesn't have to?"

"You mean—?"

I didn't get a chance to finish the thought, because he was already flagging down a very dazed eighth grade president. Poor Cap! I honestly felt sorry for him. Freshly inaugurated to an office he never ran for—well, what would you be thinking? He just wanted to get out of there and be left alone.

"Remember me, Cap? I'm Zach and this is

Naomi," Zach greeted him. "Now you know us. It's only a matter of time before you get the chance to meet everyone else in the school."

Cap's haunted eyes took in the sight of the entire student body, more than a thousand strong, streaming through the gym exits. If it hadn't been so funny—if Zach's eyes hadn't been almost turquoise—I would have confessed that the whole thing was a gag.

"I'm not good at remembering names," he told us. "I don't know a lot of people."

"We're sure you can do it," I assured him.

"One," he persisted.

"One what?"

"One person. I *see* other people—when we're in town for supplies. But Rain does all the talking."

"Rain?" I queried.

"My grandmother. She's the person I know."

That was the thing about Cap that I would never dare say to Zach. I could never escape the suspicion that *he* was putting us on even more than *we* were putting *him* on. But if that was the case, he had to be the greatest actor on the face of the earth. Because he didn't crack a smile. Not for a millisecond.

Zach pressed on with his plan, and I pressed on with mine. We put a suggestion box in the guidance office, for students to bring their concerns to the president's attention. Cap never suspected that the entries were all fake, and that we were writing them in the equipment room after Zach was done with football practice.

We spent too much time laughing for any serious romance to develop, but it was fun. We were convulsed with hysterics at the thought of our hippie asking Mr. Kasigi to convert the water fountains to Gatorade, and to erect a bullfighting stadium in the parking lot.

Surprisingly, Mr. Kasigi seemed to be kind of going along with the gag. It was one thing for him to keep out of student matters, like he did last year with that Simard kid. But when someone asks you for a bullfighting ring in an American public school, you have to know you're being pranked. Mind you, when you've just heard that same kid express the belief that a president has to know every student's name, you can never be one hundred percent sure.

Whatever the reason, our assistant principal

never took Cap aside and explained to him that someone was yanking his chain.

And we really yanked. Zach told him that he had to hold weekly press briefings for reporters from the school newspaper. The reporters? Us. We didn't work for the paper, but how was Cap going to know that?

"What about the real newspaper staff?" I asked uncertainly.

"They're not invited," Zach said decisively. "Those dweebs should be happy we didn't make any of *them* president."

The first of these conferences was held in a room that didn't exist. Cap wandered the halls like a lost soul in search of the fictional geography lab. Zach planted students out there to give him bogus directions: "Make a left at the music room, down the stairs, through the double doors, then two rights and a hard left at the furnace. . . ."

We rescheduled for Friday, after telling him how disappointed we were that he'd stood us up. He apologized and promised to do better.

This briefing was held in room 226, which did exist but was locked. While he wrestled with the doorknob, Zach sent the football cheerleaders to form their human pyramid right beside him. They chanted: *"Cap, Cap, he's our man! If he can't open it, nobody can!"*

To tell the truth, I wasn't super-high on this idea, since Lena was not only a cheerleader but also the apex of the pyramid. It was impossible to compete with anyone in a cheerleading outfit, especially at our school. Over the summer, the basement got flooded and the uniforms all shrank.

I felt better when the real press briefings began. Lena traded her pom-poms for a reporter's notebook, and we all spoke up for the people's right to know.

"Cap, what are you going to do about the terrible state of cafeteria food?"

"Cap, the boys' locker room is a cesspool! What are your plans to improve it?"

"Cap, have you thought about air-conditioning the school buses in light of global warming?"

"I don't have the answers to any of those things," was his grave reply. "Maybe you picked the wrong person to be president."

Which only proved that we'd picked exactly the *right* person to be president.

Now that Lena was back in the plan, I had to

come up with something good, in order to stand out in Zach's eyes. I invented a secret admirer for Cap named Lorelei Lumley, a seventh grade student-government groupie, who slipped perfumed love notes through the vents of his locker.

"These are perfect," Zach enthused. I could tell that he hadn't overlooked the bright-red lip imprint that I had kissed onto every piece of stationery.

Zach had Cap's combination, so we made it our mission to see that he never opened the door without finding something bizarre and/or gross. It became my favorite part of every day—pressed against Zach in the drinking fountain alcove, waiting to see what Cap would pull out of there next— a rotten banana with a greasy black peel, a goat's brain from the science lab, a Ziploc baggie of Pepto-Bismol, a dead bird.

Cap didn't react very much to any of these things, except the bird. We watched, amazed, as he wrapped the small body in a paper towel and marched it straight out the door. He got as far as the flower bed. There he knelt and began scrabbling with one hand in the soft dirt.

Zach peered through the floor-to-ceiling window. "What's he doing? Digging worms?"

"That's not it," I said in a tremulous voice. "He's burying the bird."

Zach was mystified. "Why?"

Cap placed the shrouded little corpse into the hole and covered it tenderly with earth. Then he plucked a couple of daisies and placed them across the tiny grave. He stood up, removed his psychedelic headband from that haystack of hair, and bowed solemnly.

The smart move definitely would have been to hang back with Zach and make fun of the performance. But something came over me—I still can't explain it. I walked out and stood beside Cap. I wasn't a bird lover. I didn't know a canary from a condor. But the look of sympathy on the hippie's face was so honest, so pure, that it planted the emotions inside my heart. Suddenly, I had to pay my respects to this innocent creature, cut down in the prime of life.

It wasn't much of a funeral. We stood there like junior undertakers while the wind turned Cap's unbound hair into a reasonable facsimile of a rain forest.

"Death is a part of life," he said simply. "This is just another part of your journey. Fly well."

I noticed that quite a few kids were looking on—trying to figure out if we'd gone crazy, probably. One seventh grader took off his baseball hat in reverence. I caught a disapproving look from Zach on the other side of the window, and silently cursed myself for making a mistake Lena never would have made. Yet it seemed so *right*, and I couldn't be sorry for that.

When Zach became my boyfriend, I hoped I could make him as sensitive as Capricorn Anderson.

Afterward, some of the spectators went up to Cap to say a few quiet words. He asked all of them their names.

7

NAME: **MRS. DONNELLY**

As Cap's caseworker, part of my job was to check in with the school from time to time to make sure he was doing well. That's how I wound up having lunch with Frank Kasigi, assistant principal at Claverage Middle School.

"Oh, don't worry about Cap from an academic standpoint," he assured me. "He's right up there with our brightest and best. Commune or no, he's been very well educated by someone."

I thought of Rain and shuddered, even after all these years. She had always been the teacher at Garland. For someone who rejected all forms of authority, she was a major tyrant in the classroom. If she hadn't adopted the hippie lifestyle, she would have made a terrific Marine drill sergeant.

Then Mr. Kasigi let the other shoe drop. "Yet socially—in my entire teaching career, I've never met a student who knows so little about ordinary everyday living. Have you worked with any other students from this Garland Farm?"

"Only one," I replied faintly. "She had a very difficult adjustment." I didn't bother to mention that "she" was me.

"Adjustment is one thing. But Cap is like a space traveler who just landed on Earth and left his guidebook on the home world! Is it possible that he honestly believes bullfighting is a sport we play in middle school?"

"*Bullfighting?*" I repeated. "How did that subject come up?"

His reply posed far more questions than it answered: apparently, Cap had asked about it as part of his duties as eighth grade president.

Eighth grade president? How could a brand-new student, who didn't know a soul in the place, get himself elected president?

It made no sense to me. But later on, my sixteen-year-old daughter acted like it was the most obvious thing in the world.

"Duh—eighth grade president isn't an honor, Mother. It's like being elected village idiot. Every year they pick the biggest wing nut in the building. It must have seemed like the freakazoid dropped straight from heaven to fill the post."

I was horrified. "Sophie—that's awful!"

She shrugged. "What's really awful is that you're a social worker—with power over kids' lives—and you have no clue about what's common knowledge at that school."

"Did this happen when you were in eighth grade?"

"Remember Caitlin Tortolo? She didn't really win a semester in Europe. She left school early to have a nervous breakdown."

"And you participated in it?"

"Everybody did," she retorted. "At least, we did nothing to stop it. If you don't go along with the gag, you're next." I must have looked disapproving, because she added, "Grow up, Mother. The world's a big, tough, scary place—like you don't know that."

Actually, I *did* know that. I didn't realize *she* knew it.

I felt terrible for poor Cap. It was hard enough for him to come out of total isolation at Garland without having to be dropped into the snake pit that was middle school. Worse, I couldn't even warn him about it—not without poisoning his one-and-only experience of the real world.

My sole consolation lay in the fact that he would have to suffer this abuse only for a few weeks more. His grandmother was recovering well. I'm sure he would have liked to visit her more often. But the facility was an hour away, more with traffic, and there just wasn't time to take him during the week.

Anyway, deep in my heart I believed that a genuine school, nasty and merciless as it could be, was still better than Garland Farm.

Besides, nastiness was relative. After school, Cap had to come home to my house, where Sophie was there to demonstrate the true meaning of nasty. She hated Cap Anderson with a passion that I wouldn't have believed her capable of—and I was her mother.

Even when he did things that had nothing to do with Sophie, she took them personally. His healthy vegetarian diet she considered a slap in the face to her own eating habits. His neatness was a deliberate ploy to make her appear messy. She couldn't bear that Cap woke up early to practice tai chi on our front lawn.

"But, Sophie," I tried to reason, "why would it matter to you? You're barely awake at that hour."

"It's humiliating!" she raged. "We might as well put a sign on the roof that says 'Warning: Mutant on Premises!'"

The next morning, when Cap was performing the dancelike martial arts moves by the dogwood bushes, my darling daughter emptied an entire wastebasket full of water down on his head. This she followed with a string of language that would have set fire to the sidewalk. All from the girl who was so concerned about what the neighbors might think.

He looked up at her and he smiled—instead of heaving a rock through her window, which is what I would have done. Oh, what a sight he was, with all that hair hanging limply around his shoulders. He looked like a weeping willow in soggy sandals.

According to Sophie, the entire incident was my fault. By bringing Cap into our home, I had left her no choice but to take matters into her own hands.

Since Sophie was never going to apologize to Cap, I did it myself.

"I'm so sorry, dear," I said, handing him a towel that wouldn't have dried one tenth of his abundant hair. "You have to forgive Sophie, although I can't think of a reason why."

He looked sad. "She doesn't like me."

I smiled. "Sixteen-year-old girls don't like anybody."

His answer brought me straight back to my Garland days. "When you're unkind to others, it's usually because you don't believe that you, yourself, deserve kindness."

"Don't be so nice," I said. "She can be pretty mean. In her defense, she's been through a lot in the last couple of weeks. Her father—my ex-husband— his heart's in the right place, but he makes a lot of promises he can't keep. And Sophie ends up caught in the middle. Just yesterday, she was waiting for him to pick her up for her first driving lesson. He never showed. That's him—doesn't come, doesn't call, dead air. She won't admit it, but she's devastated."

He looked thoughtful. "I guess when you have a lot of people in your life, there's more of a chance that someone will let you down."

I laughed. "You're right. But it's a risk most of us are prepared to take."

Cap looked dubious. He had grown up with exactly one person in his life—Rain. And regardless of what I thought of her, to him she had been as constant as the rising sun.

How terrifying must it be to lose that?

8

NAME: **CAPRICORN ANDERSON**

I really missed Rain.

My whole life, whenever I got confused, there she'd be to explain it all to me. One time I remember, we were in Rutherford, laying in a supply of tofu. We grew our own fruits and vegetables at Garland, but everything else had to be brought in from outside. Then we stopped at the hardware store to stock up on duct tape, which was just about the most useful thing on earth for a farm commune. It repaired roofs, walls, pipes, cars, furniture, and boots. At least a quarter of Garland was held together with the stuff. It made an instant cast for a broken finger, and even pulled splinters out of your skin. Before I was born, when there were lots of young children growing up in the community, all those diapers used to be fastened by squares of duct tape.

But when we got to the store, there was a group of people blocking the entrance. They were carrying signs and chanting. They seemed to be really angry about something.

Rain explained that the employees were on strike, standing up for fair treatment. She thought it was an excellent idea. She refused to cross the picket line, so we drove twenty miles out of our way to buy our duct tape. We came back, though, and marched with the strikers for a couple of hours. Rain even let me unscrew the knobs to let the air out of the tires of the boss's car.

Rain said the trip was the purest form of education—learning by doing. I sure could have used that kind of wisdom now, with so much going on in my life and so many things I didn't understand.

Like bullfighting. I asked Mrs. Donnelly about it, but the subject really seemed to bother her. She advised me to ignore anyone who mentioned it again. So I looked it up in the encyclopedia, and I figured out why Mrs. Donnelly was so upset. Bullfighting is a cruel sport where innocent animals are tormented, tortured, killed, and have their ears cut off.

I needed Rain more than ever to ask her why a school would have anything to do with that. But she was out of the picture. This was a decision I would have to make on my own.

And I did. The next time I saw Zach Powers, I put my foot down. "I'm not going to ask Mr. Kasigi about bullfighting anymore. I object to it on moral grounds."

He said, "I respect your honesty," and shook my hand. As he walked away, I noticed his shoulders shaking. Overcome with emotion, I guess.

I was beginning to see that growing up knowing only one other person had some serious disadvantages. Without Rain as my mentor and guide, I was lost.

The school made me dizzy. I spent half my time wandering the halls, asking people directions to rooms they'd never heard of. Students were constantly peppering me with questions I didn't have the answers to. And now a girl named Lorelei Lumley was writing me notes about how she'd love to run her fingers through my hair. Why would anybody want to do that?

The closest thing I had to Rain was Hugh Winkleman—hardly a replacement, but at least he was willing to help. We ate lunch together every day, and I found myself honestly looking forward to that regular meeting where Hugh could explain things to me.

"It's obvious," he said. "She's in love with you."

"I don't even know who she is!" I hadn't learned more than fifteen or twenty names at that point.

Hugh was disgusted. "Typical. I've spent my whole life in this dumb town, and I've never gotten a girl to give me a second look. And here you have someone named Lorelei throwing herself at you. You can't let that slip through your fingers. Ask her to the Halloween dance."

"What's the Halloween dance?"

"Only the most important social event of the school year! Not that I've ever been to one." His eyes narrowed. "If you're eighth grade president, shouldn't you know about it?"

"I hope not," I said worriedly.

Hugh looked dubious. "Well, you probably shouldn't go by me. I'm not exactly Mr. Popularity around here. But I think the president plans the whole shindig—refreshments, decorations, music—"

Something tingled directly beneath the peace sign I wore around my neck. I was developing a sixth sense for when trouble was coming my way. But what good was advance warning? Advance warning of *what*? I wasn't going to understand it anyway.

Maybe that was my mistake—even *trying* to understand. Garland was so simple—seven acres of land containing exactly one house, one barn, a vegetable garden, fruit trees, a pickup truck, and only one other person. Maybe in a place as complex as C Average Middle School, it was impossible to analyze every single thing that happened.

Like what were those little white paper balls that I kept brushing out of my hair every night? Was there so much paper in a school that the molecules eventually clustered and fell like precipitation? And how did a pickled brain and all those other weird objects get into my locker? I thought the whole point of a lock was that no one could open it but me. *I* sure never put pink goo and a dead bird in there.

Rain always recommended meditation for stress and confusion. But if you meditate in front of your locker, someone might steal your sandals while your eyes are closed.

I had to go home barefoot on the school bus that afternoon. I know complaining is a negativity trip, but it was hard to stay positive about the floor of a school bus. It's a collecting place for the filthy, smelly, sticky, and often sharp and jagged castoffs of a society run wild.

If I'd ever questioned why Rain and her friends gave up on city life in San Francisco and founded Garland back in 1967, five minutes on that bus explained it. The dark underbelly of the human animal was turned loose on that vehicle. It was crowded, noisy, dirty, rowdy, and uncomfortable. People fought, shrieked, threw things at one another, and tormented the hapless driver. It was an insane asylum on wheels.

By the time I made it to the Donnelly house, my bruised and bleeding feet were decorated with lollipop sticks, chewing gum, hairs, broken soda-can tabs, straws, buttons, and some things I couldn't even identify.

To make matters worse, Sophie caught me in the backyard hosing off my feet at the outdoor tap.

"Nice," she muttered. But the thing is, her expression said she didn't think it was nice at all. Lately, every time I talked to Sophie, she looked like she had just eaten some turnips that had been harvested a week too late. Her face twisted into an unpleasant contortion that made it hard to see how beautiful she was. But I tried my best, because I knew about her disappointment over her father and the driving lessons. I realized my good fortune at being raised by Rain, who never broke a promise and never let me down in any way.

The more I thought about it, the more I wanted to do something nice for Sophie, to make her feel better. But how could that ever happen? Every time I went near her, she practically bit my head off.

9

NAME: **SOPHIE DONNELLY**

My mother is the most generous, caring, good-hearted, sympathetic person in the world. She even chose a career devoted to helping people. She's a saint.

I always knew that lousy attitude was going to get us in trouble one day. Still, never in my wildest nightmares could I have imagined myself living with a refugee from Bizarro World.

The stuff he scraped off his feet alone would have been enough to get the house condemned by the board of health. God only knew what was living in his hair! And his clothes—I was amazed they didn't get up and walk away on their own.

Mom insisted he was very clean. I told you about her—generous to a fault.

"He's been wearing the same stuff for the past three weeks," I accused.

"They just look the same because they're all cotton tie-dyes," she explained patiently. "He has plenty of clothes. I drove out to Garland myself to pick up his things."

"I hope you brought extra shoes too," I put in. "Somebody hung a pair of corn husk sandals on the high-voltage wires by the commuter line. I wonder who they belong to. I called Brad Pitt, but he's wearing his."

"Don't be unkind," she told me sharply. "The way those kids are teasing Cap is inhuman. Have a little compassion."

"Have a little compassion for *me*," I said sulkily. "Josh was just dropping me off while the freakazoid was scraping a third-world country off his feet. You know what he said? 'Is that your brother, Sophie?'"

"What did you tell him?"

"What *could* I tell him? I said it was a homeless guy. A person can dream."

My solemn vow: should Capricorn Anderson put the kibosh on my chances with Josh Weintraub, not even Mother's social worker training could save him.

If Josh and I started dating—are you there, God? It's me, Sophie—there'd be no way to keep that space alien off the radar screen. I could have sworn there were six of him. Wherever I wanted to be, that's where he was—squeaking the porch swing, or hogging the kitchen table, eating those organic soy nuts Mom bought for him. He'd even started watching *my* favorite show, *Trigonometry and Tears*, the high-school soap opera. Because he had never seen TV before, he was a total addict who barked out warnings and advice to the characters on the screen.

"Will you shut up?" I yelled, not for the first time.

Even though he was embarrassed, he still defended himself. "Nick doesn't know that Alison found out he's been seeing Corinne on the side!"

"They're actors! It's a story! They can't even hear you!"

And he understood. Sort of. But he didn't stop talking to the TV. It was just too new to him. How would I ever explain *that* to Josh?

I needn't have worried. That relationship was

over before it started. I probably should have told Josh that Cap *was* my brother. Or maybe my husband. It would have saved me the most boring date of my life.

To think that I pulled strings and called in favors just to meet him! What a letdown. He talked about video games for three hours before telling me he was getting back together with his ex-girlfriend from Indiana. Rock on.

So I wasn't in the best of moods when Josh took me home after the ordeal. There was only one thing that could have made this night any worse— face time with My Favorite Martian.

He was waiting for me on the porch. "Hi."

"Where's my mother?"

"Around the corner at the Peabodys'," he told me. "Quick—we should have just about an hour."

I was wary. "For what? To pick a few more staples out of your feet?"

He held up the car keys and jingled them in front of me. "Driving lessons."

I stared at him. "Driving lessons? From a little squirt like you?" Then I remembered what Mom had told me—that Cap had been arrested and released for driving without a license. At that lawless flower-child Camp Day-Glo, they probably let you drive when your foot could reach the pedal without breaking the moisture seal on your training pants.

"I know your other lessons got canceled," he went on.

Oh, thanks, Mother. Someday I'll repay you by telling *your* personal business to every passing hobo.

I felt betrayed, furious—and intrigued. My father was a total flake. He'd probably get around to giving me a lesson one day, but it would be pure random chance when and if it ever happened. And Mom's killer schedule didn't leave a lot of windows of opportunity.

I wanted to drive. I *needed* a teacher. Even if it had to be the freakazoid.

I did a lot of things I'd promised myself I'd never do. I got in the car with him. I listened to him and did what he told me to do. That idiotic Zen-hippie style of his turned out to be just right for a driving instructor. No matter what mistakes I made, it didn't seem to faze Cap—not even when I thought someone's driveway was a side street and turned onto it.

"Honest mistake," said Cap, but, rattled, I

stepped on the gas instead of the brake.

The Saturn burst forward. Suddenly, a white-painted garage door loomed out of the darkness, coming up fast.

I lost it. I didn't even have the sense to take my foot off the gas. I was in mid-panic when Cap reached over and yanked on the steering wheel. We swung around, the tires of the Saturn churning soft earth as we plowed into a flower bed. The rough ride slowed us down long enough for him to reach over and shift into park. The car lurched to a halt.

"Abdominal breathing," he ordered quietly. "In through the nose, out through the mouth."

"But I almost—"

"There's no almost," he lectured serenely. "Only 'happened' and 'didn't happen.' This didn't happen."

"Get us out of here!" I whimpered when my lungs refilled with air.

"You'll do that. It's a circular driveway. Just continue around."

I was really panicking. Visions of an angry homeowner coming at us with a shotgun were whirling around my head. "I can't! It's too narrow, and there are trees on both sides! I'll hit something!" At that point, I didn't care if I never drove again. I just wanted to make it home alive in something that still resembled a Saturn.

He was endlessly patient. "This is a philosophy Rain passed on to me when she taught me how to drive our truck."

I very nearly hit him. "This is no time for your hippie-dippie wisdom!"

But there was no stopping Cap when the subject was the immortal Rain. "She said, 'If the front gets through, the rest will drag.'"

I stared at him. "That's philosophy?"

"Rain used to drive a taxi in San Francisco before she formed Garland."

I let out a nervous giggle, and it relaxed me. I put the car back in gear and aimed the hood between the two trees. May Mother never find out that I was piloting her precious Saturn on instructions from Rain, the face of so many of her childhood nightmares.

When we reached the road, I was panting with pure relief. The freakazoid made me pull over while he went back and replanted all the flowers I'd spun up. I was so grateful, I didn't even kill him.

Surviving my first brush with disaster must have

boosted my confidence, because I was a better driver after that. In short order, I was tooling around the neighborhood with something approaching skill. Pretty soon I even forgot that my learner's permit probably wasn't valid when I was in the car with someone even less qualified behind the wheel than I was.

I was so wrapped up in the experience that it took me a few seconds to recognize the female pedestrian we'd just passed.

"My mother!" I rasped. "Oh, man, we are so busted!"

He didn't seem to understand. "Why?"

"Think, for once in your life! What does neither of us have? A driver's license, maybe?" This was more serious than a few uprooted chrysanthemums. We were doing something highly illegal. "If she catches us, I'll be grounded till I'm forty, and you'll be sleeping in the street!"

For the first time, he seemed to realize that we weren't playing by hippie rules. Obviously, Mom hadn't noticed her car, because she wasn't sprinting after us, yelling. Hands trembling, I turned off the block, and we switched drivers. I may have been bugging out, but I have to say Cap was totally cool under pressure. We had to go out of our way to avoid passing Mom again. But he whipped that car around corners, through darkened streets, and up into our driveway. We sprinted in the back door, and were on the couch in front of *Trigonometry and Tears* when she came in.

She regarded me suspiciously. "What?"

I immediately grasped the weak spot in our cover. Mother had left two teenagers at war, only to return home to a peace treaty.

So I turned to Cap and snarled, "Keep your split ends off my side of the couch!"

That seemed to mollify her. It was exactly the kind of thing I'd been saying to Cap ever since he'd arrived at our house three weeks before.

But my heart wasn't in it that night.

10

NAME: **NAOMI ERLANGER**

The bad news: Lena said she didn't have the hots for Darryl *or* for Grant Tubman—at least not until the infection in his tongue stud cleared up.

The good news: she didn't come out and say she was interested in Zach. But how could she not be? He was by far the coolest guy at C Average, totally adorable, and the mastermind behind making Cap Anderson eighth grade president. Although, I have to admit I thought stealing his shoes went a little too far.

Zach didn't agree. "Come on, what kind of person sits in front of his locker, with his eyes shut, barefoot, and mumbling in some foreign language?

He was practically begging for it."

I consoled myself with the fact that they weren't even shoes. They were made out of some kind of dried leaves. Technically, we did Cap a favor, because the next day he showed up in real sneakers.

"We're bringing him into the twenty-first century," Zach insisted.

His eyes looked so sincere and so *blue* that I just had to go along with it. I couldn't help myself. I kept on writing love notes from Lorelei Lumley to slip into Cap's locker.

> Dear Capricorn,
> I waited all day and was heart-
> broken when you didn't come.
> You must have thought I meant
> storeroom B-376 of the middle
> school. Silly me, I was in store-
> room B-376 of the high school.
> There is no storeroom B-376 at the
> middle school. But I guess you
> already know that. Please, please,
> please give me another chance.
> Meet me at—

The rest was a giant tomato soup stain. I don't

know about Cap, but it would have driven *me* crazy.

Another note contained directions to a small court-yard off the library. There was only one door, and it locked as soon as it closed behind you. Poor Cap spent two hours in there, until a custodian found him and set him free. I felt pretty awful about it, but my hands were tied. I was with Zach.

We watched from a spot on the roof, expecting him to go berserk. He never did. He called for help a few times, but mostly he spent the day in the lotus position, with his new sneakers off, meditating.

I could sense Zach was a little frustrated that Cap wasn't putting on more of a show. "Why isn't he yelling? Or crying? Or at least banging on the win-dows, begging for rescue?"

To be honest, I couldn't explain it either. Cap was weird, but there was more to it than that. There was something inside him that nobody else under-stood, something mysterious and strong. Not muscle strong or fighting strong—a kind of strength that gave him the self-control to meditate instead of falling apart, or to ignore what other peo-ple thought, and find meaning in a dead bird.

I couldn't say that to Zach, of course, so I tried to be supportive. "Look on the bright side," I offered from our vantage point on the roof. "He didn't go nuts, but he was down there a really long time."

Zach was not consoled. "Yeah, and we were up *here* a really long time! What's the point of pranking someone if the prank's on you as much as on him?"

He had a point. Cap Anderson was the ultimate eighth grade president. He fell for every gag, hook, line, and sinker, more than a Luke Simard or a Hugh Winkleman ever would. There was only one problem: he wasn't reacting. You could harass him; you just couldn't upset him.

Even when Zach told him that he was expected to plan the entire Halloween dance, he was mellow about it. Last year, that was what had put Luke over the edge.

Cap just said, "I've never been to a dance."

He didn't even refuse to do it. But we knew he wasn't going to.

That made Zach mad. "We should have hung *him* off the wires, not just his sandals."

I only had one class with Cap—Math. He never opened his mouth, yet whenever the teacher called on him, he always came up with the answer. Zach claimed Cap was the dumbest kid in school, but he was really smart.

He had no friends, except maybe Hugh Winkleman, who had to be worse than nobody. Or maybe not—those two ate lunch together every single day. It looked like Hugh did most of the talking, but that made sense. Cap was new, and surely he had questions about everything that was happening to him. He had no way of knowing that the person he was using as a guide was an even bigger outcast than he was.

"So he's friends with Winkleman, big surprise," Zach sneered. "Nobody *normal* would ever hang out with him. The stuff he does—what kid in a million years would ever want to do it with him?"

He had a point. Meditation wasn't big in middle school. When Cap wasn't in the lotus position in front of his locker, he was usually in the music room, strumming a guitar and singing to himself. It was always sixties music too—I recognized the Beatles and some of the folksier stuff you hear on the classic rock stations. And every morning, he was out in the school yard, performing these slow-motion, dance-like martial arts moves. Zach called it hippie ballet, but I thought it was kind of graceful and athletic.

I asked Cap about it.

"It's tai chi," he explained. "It develops balance through a blending of mental and physical energy."

"Yeah, but why are you doing it *here*, where everybody can see you?" Zach demanded.

"Because if I do it where I live, somebody pours water on me."

You could depend on that kind of comment from Cap. It might have made sense, but only to him.

The whole thing was really starting to get on Zach's nerves. "I'm going to break this kid if it's the last thing I do."

I had to speak up. "Is this really necessary? Can't we just switch to Winkleman or something?"

"Winkleman isn't president," Zach insisted. "It's too late to go back and change that."

Anger didn't suit Zach. His jaw was stuck out, his skin flushed and taut. This wasn't the future boyfriend I'd always envisioned.

"We're eighth graders," he went on. "This is supposed to be *our year*. I'm not going to give that up because some hairy Sasquatch stepped through a time warp from the sixties!"

We went to see Lena. She was the authority when it came to spreading the word. And what

Zach had in mind amounted to calling the entire eighth grade down on Cap.

He was not to walk through a crowded hall without his feet being kicked out from under him. The cafeteria line was to become an obstacle course of tripping legs. He would be a living, breathing bull's-eye for spitballs, rubber bands, apple cores, and flying soup. It was open season on the eighth grade president, especially on the school bus, where there were no teachers, and the only rule is anything goes.

Cap's reaction? He floated through it all like he didn't even notice anyone was messing with him. No, it went beyond that—he *didn't* notice anyone was messing with him! He wasn't happy, but he didn't look unhappy either.

And here's the part I'd never admit to anyone, certainly not Zach: deep, deep down, I was rooting for Cap to stick it back in all our faces. For sure we deserved it.

Especially me, because I was starting to know better.

11

NAME: **HUGH WINKLEMAN**

This was shaping up into the greatest school year ever. True, my grades were no better than usual (straight A's), and I still couldn't climb the ropes in the gym. I was laying waste to the competition in the chess club, but that always happened. I wasn't popular, or even borderline acceptable.

But I had something going for me that was pure gold.

I was anonymous.

That may not sound like much. But to me, it was my birthday, Christmas, and the Fourth of July all wrapped into one.

No longer did I feel the ridiculing eyes boring

into me as I walked the halls of C Average. Those eyes bored elsewhere. No longer did I have to watch my step for the feet that would trip or kick me. Those feet were otherwise engaged. I could barely remember my last wedgie.

And it was all thanks to Cap Anderson.

I liked Cap. Really, I did. But I'd be less than honest if I didn't admit that the best thing about him was the fact that he took the heat off me. I was allowed to live because the pack was in full cry after him.

So I was happy, but also guilty for being happy. And the happier I got, the more the guilt spoiled my happiness.

Of all the guff I'd taken from Zach Powers over the years, this had to be the worst—that *I* was feeling bad for something *he* was doing. My only crime was *benefiting* from it. It wasn't like I could have helped Cap. If I had the power to control Zach, Lena, Darryl, and those vipers, then I wouldn't be a victim. Victims have no power. That's what makes us victims.

Anyway, this had gone far beyond just Zach's crew. It was the Luke Simard thing all over again. A wide-scale war of little attacks on Cap.

The school bus was the bloodiest battlefield. In

the building itself, there was a degree of order because there were teachers around. But on the bus the only authority was the driver, Mr. Rodrigo, and he wasn't exactly the kind of deputy you listen to. He was older, and standoffish. He kept his eyes on the road, because if he checked the mirror, he might see something. We could have held a luau on that bus, with a roast pig and hula dancers, and he would have been none the wiser.

The first projectile came sailing up the aisle, spinning like a miniature torch. The Winkleman Encyclopedia of Bullying Techniques identified it instantly. A bunch of jerks at the back were flicking lit matches at Cap.

I brushed it from the seat, genuinely alarmed. This may have been business as usual in my life, but I had short hair. Cap's flyaway mop was a forest fire waiting to happen.

Another flickering shot bounced off the armrest and extinguished itself on the floor. "Cap," I whispered urgently. "Duck."

He looked up, mystified. "Why?"

And at that very instant, Mr. Rodrigo let out a loud groan, clutched his chest, and toppled out of his seat.

The raucous clamor of the bus died as if some-one had pulled the plug. Was Mr. Rodrigo having a heart attack?

We were so frozen with shock, nobody noticed that the bus was *moving*, inching forward into oncoming traffic.

"Hey!" Cap shoved me out of the way and hit the floor running. He leaped over Mr. Rodrigo's still form and landed in the driver's seat, stomping on the accelerator. With a roar of the big motor, the bus lurched through the intersection, missing a dump truck by inches.

"Where's the hospital?" Cap barked over his shoulder.

We all sat there like dummies, scared out of our wits.

"The hospital!" Cap repeated. "Now!"

Suddenly, Naomi was sprinting up the aisle. "Turn here!"

It took all Cap's wingspan to move the huge steering wheel, swinging the bus into a tight right and speeding off down the street.

I found my voice at last. "But, Cap—you can't drive a bus!" Which was maybe the stupidest remark that could have been made. Because that's exactly what he was doing.

He shifted gears and we picked up speed. What a sight we must have been—a giant, speeding yellow school bus, weaving in and out of traffic, horn blasting.

"Turn left!" bawled Naomi.

Cap heaved on the wheel. The front tires bounced over a low concrete median, jostling passengers and rattling windows. A painful screech of metal on cement raked our ears as the chassis bottomed out. I thought we were hung up for sure, but the bus sprang forward and jolted back onto the road.

I scrambled on all fours down the aisle, maneuvering around kids who had been tossed out of their seats. Mr. Rodrigo's face was pale, but his chest was moving up and down. "He's still breathing!" I called to Cap.

All at once, the radio burst to life. "Base to forty-one," crackled the dispatcher's voice. "Come in forty-one."

Cap looked at the set as if he'd never seen one in his life—which he probably hadn't. I reached around him and took hold of the microphone. "Hello?"

"Rodrigo, is that you? We just got a report that

you're way off course and driving erratically. What's going on?"

"Uh—Mr. Rodrigo can't come to the phone—" I began.

"Who is this?" the dispatcher demanded.

"Hugh Winkleman."

"Who?"

"A passenger! Mr. Rodrigo's unconscious! We think he might be having a heart attack."

"Who's driving the bus?"

I hesitated. "Capricorn Anderson."

"Stop right there!" the voice ordered. "We'll send an ambulance for the driver."

"No," Cap told me.

"But the dispatcher said—"

"We have to get to the hospital," he interrupted. "There's no time to wait for an ambulance."

I spoke into the microphone. "He says no."

"He can't say no!" the man exploded. "He's endangering the lives of everybody on board!"

Cap glanced at the radio in annoyance. "Does this have an off button? It's very distracting."

"Uh—gotta go. Bye." I cut power to the set. To Cap I wheezed, "You sure you know what you're doing?"

"Rain says you always know what you're doing when you're doing the right thing."

About sixty seconds later, we heard the sirens.

Some kid in the last row made the identification. "Cops!"

By the time I got back there, two police cruisers were on our tail, lights flashing.

One of them activated the outside speaker. "Pull over to the side of the road!"

"You better do it, Cap!" I called. "The cops are chasing us!"

His expression was hidden behind all that hair, but he crouched lower over the wheel. It was a wordless statement—it would take an M1 tank to stop us now. I hoped this "Rain" was a reliable source. If Cap was just talking about wet weather, we were all up the creek without a paddle.

As we barreled across town in the direction of the hospital, the line of police cars continued to grow until we were leading a parade of seven black-and-whites and at least a couple of unmarked vehicles. The kids on board were totally cowed. Except for the engine noise and Naomi's shouted directions, there was utter silence. We had to be the best-behaved busload of kids in the history of C

Average Middle School. I would have enjoyed the sight of so many people who had terrorized me being terrorized themselves, except that I was twice as scared as they were.

By the time we pulled into the entrance of Metro East Medical Center, we looked like a scene from *Thelma and Louise*, with half the police department strung out in back of us in pursuit, sirens blaring. I could see nurses and paramedics diving out of the way as the big bus rocketed up the drive to Emergency. Cap stomped on the brakes, and we squealed to a halt behind a parked ambulance. A whole lot of cruisers surrounded us on all sides.

The hospital guys were angry at first, but as soon as they caught a glimpse of Mr. Rodrigo, they were all business. The fallen driver was rushed into the building on a stretcher.

No sooner had the automatic doors swallowed him up than the first officer stomped up the stairs of the bus.

"You're in a lot of trouble, kid!"

The police made Cap lie facedown in the aisle while they cuffed his hands behind his back. It was like something out of an episode of *Cops*. They were treating him like a criminal—which I guess a school bus hijacker technically was.

We watched in awe as they hauled him roughly to his feet and marched him out to a squad car.

Naomi was the first to speak up. "Cap didn't do anything wrong! He was just trying to save Mr. Rodrigo!"

The stunned passengers came alive at last. It started off as a rumbling of discontent, bubbling over into a chorus of outrage on Cap's behalf.

"Quit pushing the guy around!"

"He's a hero!"

"He didn't hit anything!"

The arresting officer wasn't buying it. "*Qui-et!!*" he bellowed. "Now, listen—I'm sending a patrolman in to drive this bus back to school. I don't want to hear a peep out of any of you in the meantime."

A door slammed as Cap was locked in the back of a cruiser. It was a terrible moment—and doubly terrible for me. Because I wasn't proud of what was going on in my head just then.

Cap had just been arrested at gunpoint; Mr. Rodrigo was in danger of his life. And what was I thinking about? That if Cap went to jail, *I* would be back in business as the number-one punching bag at C Average Middle School.

I was a worm, but at least I had the strength of character to be ashamed of it.

12

NAME: **CAPRICORN ANDERSON**

I don't think I ever would have learned to understand regular school if it hadn't been for *Trigonometry and Tears.*

It was Sophie's favorite show. I watched it with her every day after school when I didn't have something else to do, like being under arrest.

There was no TV at Garland, and it wasn't just because our generator barely had enough power to run the lights and refrigerator. Rain said television was a vast wasteland that lowered our standards until we couldn't tell the difference between bad and good. I would never disagree with Rain, but I thought *T & T* was fantastic. When I watched it, everything around me seemed to disappear, and the whole world was happening on that little screen. Those people were so *real*, with true-to-life problems and big decisions that had to be made. I kept wishing that the characters had someone like Rain to turn to in times of trouble, but they didn't. They had their parents, who were even more messed up and confused than the kids were. It was a perfect symbol for life outside Garland—huge, complicated, and full of hidden traps and pitfalls. Plus, every now and then, the program stops and the TV tells you about all the great things you can buy, like a miracle cream that makes it scientifically impossible to get a pimple.

If it hadn't been for the show, I would have been really bewildered by the huge fuss everybody was making over driving one little school bus less than five miles. The adults on *T & T* were always going bananas over something, so I wasn't surprised when the police, the superintendent, the principal, the bus company owner, and Mrs. Donnelly all took turns screaming at me. They even made Rain call from the rehab center, and gosh, it was good to hear her voice.

"I'm supposed to talk some sense into you," she

told me. "But what I really want to say is congratulations. You did the right thing."

"The police don't think so."

"Typical," she clucked. "Getting hung up on the numbers on your birth certificate when you probably saved a life."

"They made me lie on my stomach while they cuffed my hands behind my back," I complained.

"Does that bring back memories!" she exclaimed. "Every time I protested the Vietnam War, I wound up in the same position. Those were the days!"

"It was horrible."

"Don't worry, Cap," she said comfortingly. "I'm getting stronger every day. In no time at all, we'll both be back to the sanity of Garland."

Just the thought of it warmed me all over. Maybe we could get a stronger generator so we could watch *Trigonometry and Tears* there. I knew someone as smart as Rain would appreciate it if she'd just give it a chance.

I'd been doing tai chi since I was five. Rain was my teacher. She explained that if you concentrate to the point where your mind and body become one, all outward awareness melts away.

It was the first day after I drove Mr. Rodrigo to the hospital. I was halfway through my routine, when there, performing the moves beside me, was that girl Naomi. I recognized her instantly—she was one of the fifty-four names I had managed to learn so far.

"Extend your fingers," I whispered. "The energy should begin in your core and flow out through your extremities."

She made the adjustment. "Thanks."

She turned out to be a natural, but I had to cut the workout short. Zach had scheduled another press briefing for that morning. Hard experience had taught me to leave extra time to find the room.

"Well, uh, good-bye."

"Wait!" she exclaimed.

"But I have to go to a—"

"I know." She looked unhappy. Maybe she understood how difficult these briefings were for me. How I could never answer any of the questions, yet the reporters kept asking more and more.

"Cap, there's something I need to tell you."

I assumed she was going to give me directions to the journalism lab. Instead she said, "Watch out for

Zach and Lena. Watch out for all of us. We're not as nice as we pretend to be."

"You're nice," I told her.

"You're the nice one, Cap." And she ran into the school, leaving me wondering if I would ever understand people outside Garland, or if I even wanted to try.

I was a little late for the briefing because no one had heard of the journalism lab, which turned out to be just an ordinary classroom. Even more surprising, in addition to the usual reporters—Zach, Lena, and Darryl—there were at least twenty kids seated at the desks.

"Where did you learn to drive a school bus?" came the first question, from a dark-haired boy in the second row.

"Nowhere," I said honestly. Then I realized that this could be a chance to learn some new names. "And you are—?"

"Trent Davidoff."

I took out a small notepad and wrote it down. "I usually drive a pickup truck. That's why I had a little trouble on the corners."

"How did you know Mr. Rodrigo was having a heart attack?" queried the girl next to Trent.

"And your name is—?" I prompted.

"Caitlin Rankin."

I wrote that down too. "I couldn't be sure it was a heart attack. But he was lying on the floor, unconscious, and that can't be good."

A boy near the back spoke up. "What did the police say to you?" He added, "I'm Trevor Mardukas."

I scribbled it at the bottom of the page as I recalled the arresting officer's exact words. "He said, 'Keep your nose clean or next time you're looking at Juvie.'"

"Didn't you explain about Mr. Rodrigo?" asked Caitlin.

"No, I blew my nose and wiped it very carefully."

Zach was looking annoyed, which was odd. After all, these press briefings had been his idea in the first place. He raised a hand. "Is it true that you haven't even started planning the Halloween dance?"

The dance again. The entire entrance foyer was taken up with a floor-to-ceiling poster about it. There was even a picture of me, with a dialogue balloon coming out of my mouth, saying: QUESTIONS? ASK ME!

It was probably unrealistic to hope that nobody would.

"Yes, it's true," I admitted.

"Aren't you worried that you won't be ready when the time comes?" he persisted.

"I don't know anything about parties," I said honestly. "I only know fifty-seven people, including you guys."

Luckily, the bell rang, saving me from having to answer any more questions. But as we headed into the corridor, Trent approached me.

"You know, if you're looking for party music, my cousin's Bar Mitzvah had this deejay—the guy was amazing! Even the blue-hair crowd was getting down with the hip-hop moves."

I frowned. "How about the people with regular hair?"

"Kids were going nuts!" Trent assured me. "They loved it!"

I thought of something Rain once said. Back in the sixties, when Garland was a working commune, the biggest jobs went to the people who were best qualified to handle them. Why should I make decisions about a party when I'd never been to one?

I faced Trent. "You should look after the music."

He was amazed. "You're putting *me* in charge of hiring a deejay?" he asked breathlessly.

"Not 'in charge.' Authority is a power trip. A community thrives when each member does what he or she is best at. Your strength is the music."

Trent nodded. "But how do I pay the guy?"

"It's a shame that money has to enter into everything," I lamented.

"Don't worry about that," Caitlin jumped in. "The school must have a budget for the dance." She turned to me. "Right?"

I had absolutely no idea. Rain used cash to buy supplies for the commune, but I'd never even held a dollar bill in my hand. We believed that the money-crazy mind-set was a big part of what was wrong with the world.

So I said what Caitlin and Trent seemed to expect to hear: "Right."

I hoped it was the correct answer.

13

NAME: **SOPHIE DONNELLY**

The freakazoid just might be my good-luck charm. A few days after my first driving lesson, Dad resurfaced. His job involved a lot of traveling, but this time he said he was going to be around for a few months.

"So now we can see about turning you into a licensed driver." He beamed at me.

My mother gave him the Look. "Sophie was really disappointed when you didn't show up last week."

"Mother—" I said warningly. I didn't need a trained social worker nagging interference for me.

Dad chose not to pick up on the vibe. "Well, I'm

here now," he said cheerfully. "Let's go."

And we did. I have to say, I wish he was as patient as Cap. But now that our houseguest was on the cops' A-list for grand-theft school bus, it would probably be too risky to go out driving with him anymore.

Cap was doing his tai chi under the weeping willow when I maneuvered Dad's Saab into the driveway.

"God bless America!" Dad was astonished. "That's the stray your mother brought home?"

"The very same," I sighed.

"Does he have to do that right out in the open in broad daylight?"

"He used to stick closer to the house," I admitted. "I persuaded him not to. Three buckets of water did the trick." One thing about Cap—it *did* take a brick building to fall on him.

Dad laughed. "You're a saint to put up with it, Soph. This is cruel and unusual."

We agreed on that, especially the part about me being a saint. That was another advantage of having Dad around. Mom was so nice, so kind, so understanding that she made the rest of us seem like insensitive jerks. But Dad took one look at Cap

Anderson and instantly understood my side of the story. Moments like this really made me miss him when he was away, which was most of the time.

Dad waved to our houseguest as he walked me to the door. "Nice moves, kid. I used to do a little kendo in my younger days." He could make conversation with a brick wall—part of his salesman DNA.

Cap looked disapproving. "That's with swords, isn't it? Rain would never teach me anything that uses weapons."

Dad nodded in agreement. "We trained with padded sticks so no one got hurt—purely ceremonial. It was all about pressure points and energy flow. I'll show you, one of these days."

To me, he said, "Gotta run. But first—" He reached into his pocket and pulled out a small jewelry box. "—belated birthday present."

Yeah, seven months belated.

I took it from him, thrilled. It was a silver bangle, set with multicolored stones. "Love it. Thanks, Dad."

I was about to try it on when he snatched it back. "Not so fast. I just wanted to make sure you like it before I have it engraved."

Cap stared at the bracelet, hypnotized. "That,"

he said in a hushed voice, "is the most beautiful thing I've ever seen."

Leave it to him. The kid grew up surrounded by wooden planks and fertilizer—the shiniest object in his life was probably an old pitchfork. No wonder he took a few rhinestones for the crown jewels.

Dad tried to make it into a joke. "I guess you don't get out much."

"I didn't get out at all until I came here. We never left Garland except to lay in supplies."

Dad looked profoundly interested. "I forgot— you're from Garland. Sophie's mom grew up there. What's it like these days?"

There followed a description of this year's turnip crop that would have put a Tasmanian devil to sleep. Dad was classy. He looked totally fascinated by the whole thing. But every now and then he would shoot me a smirk that had me thinking sad thoughts just to keep from cracking up.

Oh, it was great to have Dad back again!

14

NAME: **CAPRICORN ANDERSON**

It was true that I now knew 129 people. But in a school of 1100, that hardly made a dent.

Rain always said, "Don't give up, and don't give in." Of course, she was talking about civil rights or protesting a war or something. But I was sure it counted for this too.

The good news was that more students were coming up to me, which was a chance for me to ask their names. Usually, they wanted to talk about the time I drove Mr. Rodrigo to the hospital. I was amazed that people seemed less interested in Mr. Rodrigo's recovery than the details of how he got to the emergency room.

Rain explained it to me the last time I spoke to her on the phone. "That's society for you, Cap. Following rules is more important than living your life. The law says you can't drive until you're sixteen. So if somebody does it, it's a huge deal. You should feel sorry for these poor kids. They're prisoners, and they don't even know it."

"That explains why Sophie is so obsessed with getting her license," I concluded.

"Exactly. What's a license? A piece of paper. That's the *real* story, Cap—that we've allowed ourselves to be enslaved by our own laws."

She was so sensible. I wish I could have talked to her twenty times a day. It was almost like I was piloting a ship through a blinding fog, and Rain was an experienced captain. I wished I could have asked her how to play every wave. But it just wasn't possible.

"Are you feeling better? When can we both go home?"

"Soon, Cap," she promised. "And in the meantime, you stay true to yourself. Don't change because everybody around you is spiritually handicapped. I don't know this Sophie girl, but her mother, Floramundi—well, let's say that she wasn't one of Garland's bigger successes. They say the apple never falls far from the tree, you know."

"Rain," I reminded her gently, "that sounds like a negativity trip."

Rain taught me that when people are negative, they're trying to put duct tape on their own damaged souls. And while we were all for using duct tape on a drainpipe or a fender, it could never hold together something as important as a soul.

"You're right," she admitted with a sigh. "It's hard to stay positive when you're surrounded by psychic zombies. I find myself slipping back to the Dark Ages before Garland. Yesterday I made a hand gesture to one of the so-called doctors—let's just hope it was muscle memory from my taxi-driving career."

It made me feel weird to hear Rain speaking ill about Sophie without even meeting her. Of course, I was partly to blame for that. I'd told Rain some of the mean stuff Sophie had said and done. I had to tell her the *good* about Sophie, but it was hard to nail down. Like when Sophie smiled, just for that instant, there was almost no such thing as sadness. Would Rain even understand that? I wasn't sure I did myself.

Everything about Sophie had a kind of shine to

it. After years of studying art with Rain, I still couldn't remember a color as intense as the glitter polish Sophie painted on her toenails. Even her shelf in the bathroom was a wondrous sight—a skyline of bottles, tubes, and jars of all shapes and hues. And the names! Passion Fruit Heel Softener with Volcanic Pumice; Bird of Paradise Exfoliating Scrub; Honey-Infused Moisturizing Lotion with Ylang Ylang. I used her Pomegranate Shampoo with Giga-Volumizing Power once, and when I looked in the mirror, I couldn't believe my eyes. My hair was standing up straight in all directions—a huge sphere of blond fuzz surrounding me like a giant halo.

I tried brushing it down, but all it did was crackle and stand even stiffer. Somehow this Giga-Volumizing Power filled your hair with static electricity as if you'd stuck your finger in a light socket.

To make matters worse, there was urgent pounding, and Sophie snarled, "Get out of there! You're hogging the bathroom!"

When I opened the door, she stumbled back three steps and gawked at me. "I've heard of bad hair days, but wow! You look like your head exploded!"

"I tried your shampoo," I confessed.

She was disgusted. "If you're going to use the Giga-Volumizer, you've got to use the conditioner that comes with it. Otherwise you might as well be pumping ten thousand volts through your hair."

I must have looked completely helpless, because she took pity on me. She grabbed a bottle, marched me to the kitchen, and shoved my head in the sink. As she wet me down with the vegetable sprayer, I could feel my hair collapsing from its planetoid shape.

"When was your last haircut?" Sophie marveled.

"I've never had one," I replied.

"Never?"

"Well, there was the time I whacked my head on the pump handle of our well. Doc Cafferty shaved part of my scalp so he could put in stitches."

She poured on some sweet-smelling stuff and started to massage it in. "Who's he? Your pediatrician?"

"No, the vet."

The massaging hands froze. "Do me a favor," she said finally. "What you just told me—never repeat that to anyone. Especially if they have Child Services on their name tag."

My hair was fine after that, and I never again used anything from Sophie's beautiful bathroom shelf. But it wasn't because she said I couldn't. She even gave me some advice about cream for oily skin. I never touched it, though. I know when I'm playing with fire.

I think she was in a better mood because her father was in town, and her driving lessons were going well. Mr. Donnelly was a really nice person, although whenever he was around, his ex-wife looked pained and squinty, like she was trying to read something off a sign that was very far away.

Mr. Donnelly even took the time to teach me some of his kendo positions. I couldn't wait to show them to Rain when we got back home.

Another reason more people were speaking to me at school was this Halloween dance.

Luckily, there was a dance on *Trigonometry and Tears*, so I sort of knew what to expect. It looked a lot like Rain's description of riots back in the sixties—hundreds of people crammed belly to belly, waving their fists and shouting. I couldn't figure out why anyone would want to do that for fun. But they did. It was all they talked about.

"I don't know what kind of food to get for the dance," I said for at least the tenth time. "I didn't even know people ate at a dance. I thought they danced."

"Yeah, but you need snacks and drinks and desserts," said Holly van Arden (No. 130). "My neighbor goes to St. Andrews, and at their last prom, they had Create-Your-Own-Pizza. You design the pie, toss the dough, add the toppings, and it cooks while you're dancing. People are still raving about it."

"Well, I think we should have that," I decided. "Go ahead and set it up."

"It's not cheap," she warned. "They have to bring in these giant ovens on wheels."

I told her what Rain told me when I asked what would happen if we weren't able to afford our monthly trips for supplies. "When you spend your life worrying about money, pretty soon money *becomes* your life."

"Cool!" she exclaimed. And she took on the job.

In the identical way, people volunteered to handle drinks, desserts, posters, and decorations.

The next morning when I arrived at school to do my tai chi, Holly van Arden asked if she could join me. Naomi was already waiting for us.

15

NAME: **HUGH WINKLEMAN**

Cap's best friend.

I was surprised when I overheard someone calling me that. Not that I had a problem with it. When people discussed me, the sentence usually began with "The biggest dork in the whole school is . . ." *Friend* had to be a promotion from that.

And it was true. Well, true-ish. If anybody was his friend around here, I was. We spent a lot of time together, but only at school. For all I knew, he stepped off that bus every afternoon and was *whooshed* into Dimension X—which might have explained a thing or two about his personality.

I tried to take the friendship further a couple of

times, but he didn't want to join the chess club—he gave me a whole speech on the evils of competition. And when I invited him over to my house, he just said no. He wasn't being rude; he was just being Cap. Obviously, I couldn't invite myself to the place where he was staying, since that wasn't really his home.

Okay, I figured, how about neutral territory? Maybe I could coax him into a trip to the mall.

"That's a really cool shirt," I told him. "Where did you buy it?"

Another dead end. "Rain and I do our own tie-dying at the community." Then he caught me off guard. "Do you want me to teach you?"

Breakthrough.

We reconvened the next morning in the art room before classes. I brought a couple of plain white T-shirts, and Cap showed me how to scrunch, twist, and tie them up, securing them with rubber bands. Then he rummaged through the cabinets and took out enough chemicals to create a small nuclear bomb. Well, not really, but it was a lot of stuff—mostly paints and dyes, and solutions to make the colors permanent.

We were dipping the first shirt in a tub of purple when Miss Agnew came in to get ready for first period. Uh-oh, I thought, we'll be finishing this job in detention.

"Hugh Winkleman, I hope you've got permission—" Her eyes fell on my partner in crime. "You're Capricorn Anderson! I heard about what you did for Mr. Rodrigo. You're a hero!" She peered into the sink. "Wow, tie-dying! I haven't done that since college!"

When Miss Agnew's first period class showed up at the bell, they found the three of us up to our elbows in color and wet fabric. She sent them back to their lockers for T-shirts and gym shorts—anything that would take paint.

"But I thought we were drawing the human figure in motion," said one seventh grader.

"Tomorrow," Miss Agnew promised absently. "Today we tie-dye."

She even called down to the office and got Cap and me excused from period one so we wouldn't get in trouble. But I guess the conversation didn't stop there, because a few minutes later, an announcement came over the PA:

"Those students interested in tie-dying with eighth grade president Capricorn Anderson should report to the art room."

Well, what self-respecting middle school kid would turn down a free pass to get out of work? We were mobbed in there. People were lined up with their towels, socks, underwear, and any canvas bag that was supple enough to be twisted and tied. Miss Agnew was in her glory. Never before had her art room seen such enthusiasm.

The star of the show was definitely Cap. He was demonstrating, helping, mixing colors, and hanging up finished work. This was more than just Tie-Dye Palooza. Kids were asking him about the bus-driving incident and the Halloween dance, and hanging on his every word. It hit me then—everybody had seen Cap at the assembly, and around the halls here and there, but no one really knew him. Today had started out as my attempt to get a couple of shirts tie-dyed and hang out with Cap in the process. Yet before my eyes, it had turned into the eighth grade president's coming-out party. There must have been eighty students in that room, and I'll bet ninety-five percent of them approached him at some point.

True to character, he asked all their names and wrote them in his notebook.

For the rest of the day, the halls were ablaze with

color as the artists proudly wore their creations, most of them still wet. It was a carnival atmosphere, with lots of pointing and laughing and high fives.

Which might explain why I almost didn't notice something else that was different about today: there wasn't a single spitball lodged in Cap Anderson's hair.

Not one.

16

NAME: **CAPRICORN ANDERSON**

I knew something was wrong the minute I got off the bus and walked to the Donnellys'. The Saturn was in the driveway, which meant that Mrs. Donnelly was home early. And the TV was off, even though *T & T* would be on in a few minutes.

Sophie and her mom were in the kitchen. I heard Mrs. Donnelly's voice first:

"Oh, honey, don't feel bad. You know how he is."

I hurried into the room. "What happened? Is everything all right?"

An empty Dasani bottle missed my ear by inches. "Get out of here!" Sophie shrieked. "Mind your own business!"

"Sophie!" her mother exclaimed in horror. "You apologize to Cap!"

In answer, she leaped out of her chair and raced for the stairs. "Mother, don't you dare tell the freakazoid anything about this!" She pounded up to her bedroom and slammed the door.

I looked at Mrs. Donnelly. "What did I do?" It was a silly question. What did I ever do? Nothing. And Sophie still treated me as if I'd crawled in from the septic tank.

"Please forgive Sophie," Mrs. Donnelly begged. "She's just had some bad news."

I was worried. "Did something happen to Mr. Donnelly?"

"Nothing that hasn't happened before," she sighed. "He took off without so much as a good-bye."

"But what about the driving test?" I protested. A license might have been just a piece of paper, but to Sophie it meant everything.

She shrugged. "We'll just have to reschedule for when I can take her. My ex-husband is not a terrible person, but he doesn't see things through. He rolls into town, gets everybody's hopes up, and then he's gone until the next time, when he does it all over again. I learned my lesson and got off the roller coaster. My daughter hasn't figured it out yet."

I felt terrible for Sophie. She was really crushed. Mr. Donnelly left town so suddenly that she hadn't even gotten her bracelet back from the engraver. Who knew if she'd ever see it again? But, of course, it was a lot more than losing a silver bangle that upset her.

Life certainly gets complicated when you know more than one person. I could only imagine what it would be like when I knew eleven hundred.

On *Trigonometry and Tears*, there was a character named Rishon, who really bothered me. He didn't cheat on his girlfriend like Nick, or spread computer viruses just for fun like Aurora. But his irresponsible behavior was almost impossible to bear.

Sophie definitely didn't agree. "What do you care? It's a TV show." Her mood had been in free fall since Mr. Donnelly's departure.

"But if he doesn't retake the SAT to bring up his score, the University of Florida is going to withdraw his acceptance!" I exclaimed.

She looked at me pityingly. "So?"

"He hasn't even started studying! And he over-slept and missed the practice test!"

"That's what they do on *T & T*," she explained. "They take perfectly normal people and turn their lives into pond scum. That's why it's fun to watch. If everything was perfect, there'd be no story."

"But what's Rishon going to do next year?" I persisted.

"Probably find a part on a different show. He's an actor."

Because Sophie had been watching TV her whole life, and not just a few weeks like me, it was easier for her to watch Rishon throw his whole future away. For me it was agony.

Rain always said that when we judge others, we're really judging ourselves. That was the real reason Rishon upset me. How could he think his SAT scores were going to go up by themselves? How could he ignore the fact that he was about to lose his spot in college?

It was all too familiar. As eighth grade president, I was in charge of the Halloween dance, and I was giving it the Rishon treatment. I was ignoring the whole thing, almost as if I thought it might go away.

Then, on *T & T*, it all worked out for Rishon.

One of Aurora's viruses found its way into the admissions department computer at the University of Florida, wiping out half their records. All that were left indicated that Rishon was accepted. He ignored his problem—and the problem just sort of melted away.

With a growing sense of wonder, I realized that the same thing was happening with the dance. I was still doing nothing, yet somehow, the arrangements were being made. Students would come up to me in the halls; they would sing along when I played guitar in the music room; they would join in my morning tai chi routine—and then they would volunteer to help. So many people were working on the party that I was beginning to think we were actually going to have one.

No wonder *T & T* was such a popular show. It was practically an instruction manual for life.

Garland Farm followed simple logic: you plant tomato seeds, you get tomato plants. No seeds, no tomatoes. Cause and effect. But a real school was so messy and random that solutions sometimes fell into place by sheer luck. It was almost like getting tomatoes without first planting seeds.

I thought I'd never get used to the outside world,

with its chaos and clutter. But with millions of puzzle pieces being tossed up into the air, it really did stand to reason that the occasional one would come down in the right place. That was why Rishon would go to college, and C Average would have its Halloween dance.

Even Rain would have to admit that there was something kind of impressive about that.

"Anderson—come over here! I need a word with you."

The words jolted me out of deep meditation. I looked up to see Mr. Kasigi glaring down at me.

"Why haven't you come to meet with me yet?"

I was floored. "I did—the day I registered."

"Don't play dumb with me, mister! I'm hearing talk of deejays and pizza ovens on wheels! How were you going to pay for all that?"

"I don't have any money."

He was getting red in the face. "Nobody expects *you* to pay for it! The school has money set aside for the dance. But if you don't present your budget, I can't release one penny!"

"I don't have a budget," I explained honestly. "I just have people who help me do things."

"Like what? Fix your cuckoo clock?" He launched into a long speech about how he had volunteered to be on the program committee for some principals' conference, so he didn't have time to nursemaid me through Finance 101, whatever that was.

"But it's all taken care of," I tried to tell him. "The food, the music, the decorations—it all just worked out." I stopped myself before telling him about Rishon. I had a feeling Mr. Kasigi was not a *T & T* fan.

"And who's writing the checks?" he demanded.

"Checks?"

Rain had a checkbook, but I never saw her touch it. "Sometimes we use money to get along," she used to tell me, "but that doesn't mean we have to become its slave." To Rain, financial matters were a distasteful but necessary private function, like going to the bathroom.

Mr. Kasigi said I would have to write checks. Not only that, but he would have to cosign them or they wouldn't count.

After school, he drove me to the bank. I'd never been in one before. But the instant I stepped inside, I knew this was a place that represented everything

Rain and I were rejecting by living at Garland. Money was all that was important here. People were depositing it, withdrawing it, borrowing it, and paying it back. They were counting it in broad daylight. I honestly felt like running away.

But how could I? For one thing, there was a man in uniform guarding the door. I practically jumped out of my skin when I realized that he had a great big gun strapped to his hip.

Mr. Kasigi noticed my reaction. "Calm down, Anderson. He's a security man, not a bank robber."

Every time I thought I was fitting into my temporary life, something would remind me just how much of an outsider I still was. I wanted less than nothing of what this place had to offer. But to people outside Garland, money was so desirable that the bank had to hire armed guards to keep criminals from stealing it. When I finally got back home, I was going to drop to my knees and kiss the ground.

Mr. Kasigi and I met with an assistant manager. And when it was all over, I was holding a book of checks marked Claverage Middle School: Student Activity Fund.

"You'll need these to pay for music and food," he explained, signing the first twelve checks on the spot. "And I'm sure there will be other expenses that come up. They always do."

I tried to tell him that I didn't know the deejay *or* the pizza company—that other students had made the arrangements. But he interrupted me with this long lecture about how this money belonged to everybody, not just me, and how I had to be responsible. And I would have been—if I had the slightest idea what he was talking about.

All I wanted was for him to leave so I could get out of this awful place. I wouldn't even let him drive me to the Donnellys'. I needed to walk there in the fresh air, just to get the smell of banking out of my nostrils.

A few blocks down the street, a sight met my eyes that stopped me in my tracks. There, in the display window of a small jewelry shop, gleamed a silver bangle with multicolor stones. It was exactly the same as Sophie's birthday gift from her father— the one he'd taken for engraving and never brought back.

I stepped into the store for a closer look. It was beautiful, but also kind of sad, because it reminded me of how upset Sophie had been lately.

The idea came immediately. If I bought this

bracelet, had it engraved, and sent it to Sophie, she'd never know that it hadn't come from her father. And it would make her happy.

I didn't have any money. But I had something even better—checks, which automatically counted as exactly as much money as you wrote in that little box. It probably wasn't what Mr. Kasigi had in mind. But I remembered his exact words: *Be responsible*.

Rain always said that nothing was more responsible than doing what was in your power to make another human being happy.

"I'll take it," I told the woman behind the counter.

"It's a hundred and seventy-five dollars." She was wary.

"Do you accept checks?"

17

NAME: **MRS. DONNELLY**

I left four messages for Frank Kasigi before he finally called me back.

He was apologetic. "Sorry, Flora. You know I'm chairing the principals' conference this year, and it's just details, details, details."

"Sorry to bother you when you're so busy. I thought I'd better check up on Cap Anderson. Has he been fitting in any better?"

"Fitting into what?" he asked. "The Age of Aquarius?"

I felt my heart sink. "That bad, huh?"

"Actually, not really. I had the boy pegged as a train wreck. But considering how odd he is, and how sheltered his life has been, things could be a lot worse."

"He has friends?" I asked hopefully.

"Not friends, exactly. More like followers."

"Followers?"

"Ever since that stunt with the school bus, the kids just flock to him. He put together a tie-dying clinic with the art teacher. You wouldn't believe the turnout! It was"—he chuckled—"what did they call big events back in the sixties?"

"A happening," I supplied automatically.

"Right. And that's the least of it. He picks up a guitar in the music room and strums a few old Beatles tunes, and pretty soon he's got twenty people in there singing along. He's running some kind of martial arts class on the front lawn. He's got more kids working on the Halloween dance than will probably come that night. He's even got a few meditators. If I didn't know the kid's history, I'd probably have the police making sure he wasn't setting up a cult."

It triggered an explosion of images from my own childhood at Garland. Cult was exactly the word for it, with Rain as its philosopher/guru.

Still, the news made me breathe easier. "That's a

load off my mind. When I found out they made him eighth grade president—well, Sophie filled me in on what that might mean."

"I've heard those rumors too," he admitted. "It certainly hasn't gone smoothly for the last few in that office. But we don't want to be the only middle school in America with no student government. So we threw the dice, and this time we lucked out."

"Thank heaven." But maybe I should have realized that Cap was holding his own in his new life. He was still a fish out of water, but he didn't seem to be quite so thrown by every little thing as he had been when I'd first brought him home.

One major clue was the fact that he was taking a genuine interest in that school. As a social worker, I kept current yearbooks from all the buildings in my district. Not only was Cap borrowing the Claverage books, but he was spending hours studying them. Imagine, a boy who had never had even a single classmate now wanting to know about more than a thousand of them. I found it heartwarming.

Things were even thawing slightly between Cap and my daughter. Mind you, that had more to do with a change in Sophie than a change in Cap. She was in a better state of mind because her father had finally remembered to send back her extremely belated birthday present, duly engraved.

Truth be told, I'd never expected to see it again, and I don't think Sophie had either. So imagine my surprise when she opened a padded mailer with no return address and pulled out that silver bangle. There was no card, not even a scribbled note. The only thing that spoke for this gift was the engraving on the inside of it:

ALL YOU NEED IS LOVE

To be honest, the inscription threw me a little. It certainly didn't sound like the Bill Donnelly I used to be married to. His idea of sentimentality was the presentation of the Lombardi trophy at the end of the Super Bowl. But I guess he could still surprise me. He certainly got this one right. Sophie was thrilled.

It almost made up for the fact that he had walked out of her life yet again.

Even with the new, kinder, gentler Sophie, Cap was still a whole lot nicer to her than she was to him. He probably had a crush on her. An attractive high school girl had to look good to an eighth grader, especially one who had barely laid eyes on a female who wasn't his grandmother.

I couldn't prove that, of course. But one day, I came home from work, and the two of them were on the couch in front of *Trigonometry and Tears*, that awful teen soap opera geared to the interest level of chimpanzees and various species of plant life. A steamy make-out scene was taking place on the screen. Sophie was watching it intently. And, more to the point, Cap was watching Sophie. He was a difficult one to read, but I believed he was trying to work up the guts to lean over and put his arm around her.

So I slammed my briefcase down on the kitchen counter and said the first thing I could think of: "Who's up for a nice tall glass of lemonade?"

"Mother!" Sophie exclaimed in exasperation. "What century is this?"

I told myself I was protecting my daughter. But the truth is, I was protecting Cap from what Sophie would have done to him if he'd made a move on her.

The pain of my own adjustment from Garland was decades in the past. But it felt like yesterday when I watched this poor boy. I took Frank Kasigi at his word when he said Cap was doing well. But I knew I wouldn't sleep at night until he was once again with Rain, hobbling back toward the sixties as fast as her pinned hip would carry both of them.

18

NAME: **HUGH WINKLEMAN**

I was the first dropout from Cap's morning tai chi group. Literally.

Not that I'd ever been the star of the class. Two left feet weren't exactly an asset in martial arts. But I was Cap's friend—as much as it was possible to get close to someone like him. I wore my tie-dyes proudly, secure in the knowledge that I had more right than anybody. After all, who hung out with Cap *before* he ever drove a bus, or masterminded a dance?

So there I was, waving my arms and hopping around like a turkey amped up on Mountain Dew, when the planted foot was kicked out from under me. It was so sudden, so devastating, that to this day, I have no idea who did it to me. Darryl Pennyfield is my prime suspect, because he was close by, but I didn't catch him in the act. One minute I was upright—the next, I was on the grass, rolling. To the other kids in the group, it must have looked like I'd just vanished into thin air.

Were my deepest, darkest fears coming true? This was a great school year because Cap was taking the heat off me. But he wasn't a target anymore. Target, heck, he was practically a celebrity! It was the bus-driving thing that started it. When your whole world is a cheesy, prepackaged rehearsal for being alive, like middle school, a kid your own age who can pilot a twenty-ton bus is impressive. Plus the fact that he saved somebody's life, obviously. Now people were treating the eighth grade president like—well, like an eighth grade president. Someone who was admired and popular, a student leader who took an active role in the school.

And that was great—for Cap. But what did it mean for me? Was I back in the crosshairs because he was out of them? Only time would tell.

Of all the newly minted Cap fans, the biggest surprise had to be Naomi Erlanger. She was with that whole Zach Powers crew, and not as a hanger-on either. She was part of the inner circle, Lena's best friend. That was royalty around here.

Needless to say, I didn't know her well. Steering clear of that crowd was a good way to avoid being dangled by my ankles over a toilet bowl. But I'd heard that she had a big crush on Zach. And let's face it, if the rumor had made it down to my lowly rung on the ladder, you had to figure it was all over the school.

So what was her sudden fascination with Cap? She was star pupil of his tai chi group; she was constantly turning up at his locker to show him a new peace-sign bracelet she'd bought, or a magazine article on Vietnam or the Beatles or anything about the sixties. Come to think of it, hers had been the first face at the door after the PA announcement on tie-dying day. The eighth grade wing was on the opposite end of the building from the art room. She must have sprinted the entire distance.

Of course, she was still one of the beautiful people. So when I spotted her, flanked by Lena and Darryl, coming our way in the hall, I was on my guard.

"Hi, Cap," Naomi greeted us. Another thing about Naomi: I was invisible to her. Either that or I was like Cap's pet ferret—a subhuman companion, undeserving of attention. "We're walking in the March of Caring this weekend, and we need sponsors."

Darryl looked me up and down, a threatening expression on his face. "It's for a really good cause."

I pulled a pair of crumpled dollar bills from my pocket. It made no difference to me if the money was going to support throwing puppies off thirty-story office towers. This wasn't a charitable donation. I was purchasing wedgie insurance, and Darryl was Allstate.

"Sorry it can't be more."

With a grunt of acknowledgment, Darryl snatched the money out of my hand and passed it on to Lena.

Naomi's worshipful eyes never left the eighth grade president. "What do you say, Cap?"

He took out the checkbook and began writing on it.

I frowned. "Isn't that the school's money?"

"Mr. Kasigi said spend it responsibly. What could be more responsible than giving to charity?"

"Paying for the dance," I replied. "That's what it's supposed to be for."

He was serene. "I've been inside that bank, Hugh. They've got plenty of money for everything." He tore off the check and handed it to Naomi.

She took one look at it and let out a shriek that raised the roof clean off the school.

Lena gawked over her shoulder. *"A thousand dollars?"*

"What?" I wheeled on Cap. "Are you *nuts*? You can't give away that much!"

"Rain says there should be no limit on giving," he lectured serenely. "Only taking."

"She's not the one Mr. Kasigi's going to *strangle*—"

But my words were lost in the excited buzz as students flocked around to investigate the source of Naomi's scream. Lena took the check from her and held it up for the crowd. There were oohs and aahs.

"You're awesome, Cap!" Naomi cried emotionally. "Awesome!"

Darryl nodded fervently. "You're the man!"

Suddenly, everybody was clapping and cheering. I was blown away. Not one of those idiots had the faintest idea that Cap's donation came straight out of the budget for the Halloween dance.

I wanted to scream: *Look at the check! The school's name is printed right on it! This money is yours—mine—all of ours!*

That was when I experienced a moment of stunning understanding. Popularity had nothing to do with the truth. If these kids took a minute to ask themselves where Cap got off writing thousand-dollar checks, they'd be rioting, not applauding. But what really mattered was image. The eighth grade president was a star now. Nobody questioned it when he did something wonderful, because that's exactly what was *expected* of him.

All the adulation must have been overwhelming to someone like Cap, who was so accustomed to peace and quiet. He pushed his way through a barrage of high fives and ducked into the bathroom. I followed him, struggling with my own feelings about this. I wanted to be happy for the guy, but why? Because he did something stupid? His entire rise to fame seemed bizarre. Random. Dumb.

"Must be nice," was all I could think to mutter.

"It *is* nice," he agreed in wonder. "I couldn't have imagined how good it feels when so many people like you."

I recoiled as if he'd slapped me. Being liked was

a feeling I didn't know. That I might never know. And to have that rubbed in my face by my one kindred spirit, the only person around who was more of an outsider than I was—it was the ultimate insult.

I didn't care if he grew up on Pluto, let alone some hippie commune. To say that to *me*—someone who'd never experienced a popular *minute*, much less a popular day—was beyond cruel. Nothing could have made me feel worse than I did at that instant.

The door was flung mightily open, and into the boys' room burst Naomi, her face pink with daring. She threw her arms around Cap and pressed a long kiss right on his mouth.

Cap was so shocked that he crumpled against the stall door when she let go.

"To be continued," she said meaningfully, and ran out of the bathroom.

I glowered at him through eyes that were barely slits. Hero status wasn't good enough for him anymore. He had to be a heartthrob too.

I was finished with Capricorn Anderson.

19

NAME: **ZACH POWERS**

I saw a show last night with a bunch of scientists arguing over what the signs will be when the world is coming to an end. They talked about asteroids, volcanoes, and melting ice caps.

Small minds.

When Cap Anderson becomes the most popular, happening kid at C Average Middle School, *that's* the end of the world. Especially when you consider that the guy he replaced was *me*.

It was all because of that stupid dance. How could a hippie who knew less than nothing about parties organize the middle school bash of everybody's dreams?

"It's your own fault," Lena accused. "You recruited half the school to bug him, and he turned them into an army of volunteers."

She had a point. With the exception of me and the Hairball-in-Chief, *everyone* was working on the Halloween dance—even the cool people. Darryl was hauling huge rolls of construction paper to the decorations people in the art room. Naomi was designing reflective mobiles to hang from the basketball hoops. Lena was on the committee to cover the bleachers with orange-and-black bunting. Even cheap paper chains were impressive when you had eleven hundred kids stringing them.

"This is going to be the greatest party we've ever had!" Naomi enthused. "I'll bet we get a thousand kids."

"And that's just the planning committee," I added sourly.

"What's wrong with that?"

"Ignore him," Lena put in. "He's in mourning because he thinks Cap stole his year."

"*Our* year," I corrected. "And he's making it into 1967!"

"You shouldn't be so hard on Cap," Darryl told me. "Sure, he's weird, but he's the best eighth

135

grade president we've ever had."

"Eighth grade president isn't a real job," I seethed. "It's a joke, remember?"

"Well, maybe it started that way," Naomi said earnestly. "But Cap Anderson is the most amazing person I've ever known."

I snorted. "Anybody can be amazing handing out thousand-dollar checks."

Now *that* had caught me off guard. What was up with all this charity? He gave eight hundred to the food drive in the cafeteria. Five hundred to cancer research. The same to Alzheimer's disease. They may have called it the March of Dimes, but that didn't stop Cap from forking over six-fifty. He even stuck checks into the slots of those cans designed for people to drop their spare change.

Mr. Kasigi had to be behind it somehow. Cap wouldn't be allowed to throw around big chunks of school money without permission from the office. Maybe the whole thing was a lesson about philanthropy. It bugged me. The eighth grade president wasn't supposed to set a good example. His job was to make an idiot out of himself and have a nervous breakdown. But no, the assistant principal had to set Cap up for sainthood!

Whatever Kasigi was thinking—*if* he was thinking—I was the one paying the price. I was spending more and more of my time arguing with my friends, and all because of that hairball.

My year. Yeah, right. More like my minute.

How do you think I felt at lunch on Tuesday when I walked out of the food line with my tray and found Cap Anderson at *my* table, in *my* seat? Okay, it was a big cafeteria, but I'd been working my way up to that position since the very first day of sixth grade. It hadn't taken me more than thirty seconds to look around the room and know that this was the place where the masters of the universe ate their tuna fish sandwiches. It was near the wall of windows, but not so close as to get too hot on sunny days. Yet, at the end of the period, a shaft of light always seemed to shine down like a spotlight on the person sitting in the end chair. *My* chair—at least until today.

Those filtered rays were shining now on the haystack of Sasquatch hair. I stared at Darryl. The gutless wonder wouldn't even look me in the eye. He was concentrating on the exit sign over the door, which may or may not have been a message for me to get out. Naomi was focused on Cap, which meant nobody else in the building existed. Lena was the only one with the nerve to face me. Her look plainly announced that not only had I lost my spot, but I wasn't welcome to pull up a chair and squeeze in either.

Fuming, I turned away.

Crash!

It was a tray-to-tray collision. My split pea soup sloshed onto his egg-salad sandwich; his Tater Tots flipped into my banana cream pie; his Snapple tipped over, raining down on my shoes.

I stared at the idiot as iced tea soaked into my socks. The last person I wanted to see just then.

Hugh Winkleman.

He stood frozen with fear, probably straining all those math brain cells to calculate how big a wedgie he'd just earned himself. Let me tell you, he should have been thinking huge. I had half a mind to stick a booster rocket under his waistband and launch it into orbit.

"You—"

And then I took in the expression on his face, and it was like looking in a mirror. He was staring at his hippie friend, who now had no time for him. And I was staring at my friends—same story.

In a way, it was more depressing than anything that had happened so far. I, Zach Powers, had something in common with this loser. That had to be rock bottom.

Still, there was only one other person in the whole school who was as disgusted as I was by all this hippie-mania. And that person had just dropped his lunch on me.

"Uh—sorry," he said nervously.

I felt an odd rush of emotion. It wasn't affection, trust me. But Hugh represented an earlier time at this school—before the space capsule landed and barfed up Cap Anderson. A time when things made sense.

Hugh was the one who should have been eighth grade president all along. Heck, if I'd met Cap twenty-four hours later, it probably would have happened exactly that way. Then this would still be my year, and Cap would be nothing more than a walking bad-hair day nobody really knew.

"Don't worry about it," I told Hugh. "Listen— we've got to talk."

He looked so suspicious that I felt a pang of remorse for the mean things I'd said and done to him since kindergarten. In all the years I'd known him, we'd never had a conversation that hadn't been a sham to lure him through a door with a bucket of ice water balanced on top. Sure he was suspicious. Wouldn't you be?

"About Cap Anderson," I elaborated, "and everything that's been going on."

Hugh expanded his tunnel vision on Cap to include an inventory of the guy's tablemates. He sneered at me. "Oh-ho-ho! Looks like somebody's been replaced!"

I swallowed my pride. "You'll notice Cap isn't hanging with you anymore."

"I was his friend when no one else would talk to him," Hugh said resentfully. "When you and your cronies were trying to ruin his life."

"Well, whatever we were plotting, it obviously didn't happen. He's practically the king of the school."

Hugh nodded slowly. "I don't like it either."

"It doesn't have to be this way," I pressed on.

He rounded on me. "You are such a *jerk*! Whoever told you that the whole world performs according to your instructions? That's what started this whole mess—you trying to make poor Cap dance to your tune!"

"I don't remember you warning the guy off when we nominated him for eighth grade president," I snarled.

"Because I was grateful the nominee didn't turn out to be *me*."

I pounced on this. "So you let Cap swallow the hook. Now who's the manipulator? You're just as guilty as I am."

"Maybe so, but I'm not stupid," he said hotly. "Making Cap your victim blew up in your face. Now you want him out so you can stick me in his place."

"It's not like that," I pleaded. "Look, Cap's president. We're stuck with that. But there's still time to puncture the tires of this bandwagon before the Halloween dance ratchets him up to icon status."

"No way! Just because I'm mad at Cap doesn't mean I'm going to help you stab him in the back!"

At *my* table, Naomi leaned over and dabbed delicately at a ketchup smear on the side of Cap's mouth. I almost upchucked. "Will you look at that!"

Hugh had been watching too, his face twisted with distaste. He said, "To be continued."

"What's that supposed to mean?"

"Nothing," he muttered, not quite meeting my eyes. "What do you need me to do?"

I shrugged. "Simple. The whole school thinks he's immortal. We just have to show them they're wrong."

20

NAME: **CAPRICORN ANDERSON**

I don't remember exactly when I stopped keeping count of how many people's names I knew. It was somewhere in the three hundreds, and the total had to be even higher now.

The yearbooks made the biggest difference. I'd look at those little black-and-white pictures, and suddenly an image of someone I'd seen around school would pop into my head. And *poof*, I'd know another student.

I was kind of lagging behind on the sixth graders because they weren't in the C Average yearbook. But Mrs. Donnelly had the elementary books as well. And there they were—the graduating fifth-grade class.

Rain would be proud. I used the memory technique she had learned from a college professor who'd passed through Garland in the early seventies. You find a connection between the name and something about the person. For example, Monique rhymes with streak, and she had a blond streak in her dark hair. Darryl was built like a huge barrel. But sometimes I had to be a little more creative. Seventh-grade Ron had a birthmark shaped like a crab, which made me think of the Crab Nebula. AstRONomy. It sounds difficult. But once your brain is used to working that way, it happens almost automatically.

For someone who grew up knowing only one person, suddenly knowing hundreds of them was a little intimidating. But I had to admit it was kind of wonderful too.

In Sophie's opinion, studying old yearbooks was just another reason why I had to "get a life." Of all the things she said to me, this was maybe the most baffling. How could I get a life when I was obviously already alive?

We were seeing less and less of each other, despite the fact that we were in the same house. Sophie's driving test was in a week, so she never passed up a chance to practice with her mother. And she wasn't watching TV with me anymore because *Trigonometry and Tears* had gone into reruns, which meant they were showing old stories that we'd already seen.

I thought it was fantastic, because it gave you another chance to notice things you might have missed the first time around.

She rolled her eyes at me. "We just saw this episode two weeks ago. Lashonda flunks home ec and gets caught lending Troy's letter jacket to that college guy she's been dating on the side."

I wished she hadn't said that, because I wanted to be surprised again, even though I knew it was going to happen.

But she'd been fairly upbeat lately. She was excited about her road test, and so happy with her bracelet. I was thrilled that I'd been able to do that for her.

The best thing about being eighth grade president was definitely the checks Mr. Kasigi had given me. It was funny—a money-obsessed world was the main reason Rain had dropped out and formed Garland. Yet, in my experience, money was really excellent, and every time I spent it, someone ended up smiling.

I was planning to mention it the next time Rain and I spoke on the telephone. Money could help hospitals and disaster victims and starving orphans. What was so terrible about it? Thanks to Mr. Kasigi's checks, I was in a position to lend a hand. It was everything she had taught me to believe in.

Mr. Kasigi would be back from his conference next week. I couldn't wait to show him how good I'd become at using money. Also, I needed some more checks. The first batch was almost finished.

He was going to be impressed.

C Average Middle School had three lunch periods of forty minutes each. On Wednesday, classes were canceled during that two-hour block so everyone could go to the football field.

Hugh explained it to me. "It's a pep rally."

"Pep?" I repeated.

"You know, cheering, excitement, rah, rah, rah. The whole school gets together to watch the players bonk helmets and beat their chests."

"And that takes two hours?" I queried. I was getting better at understanding school customs, but this one didn't make much sense to me.

"Not really," Hugh admitted. "Most of that time

is getting everybody in and out again. But it's pretty intense. We play Rhinecliff on Saturday, and they're our biggest rivals."

"Over what?"

"Football, of course. And as the eighth grade president, you have an important role."

Rain and I weren't sports fans, what with the obsession over winning and losing. But I couldn't disappoint everybody after they'd made me feel so welcome.

I followed Hugh into the mass migration of students heading out of the building at eleven fifteen. We were a noisy procession, with horns and cowbells and excited voices chanting rhyming cheers.

It was hard not to be swept up in it, even though I wasn't sure what it was about. So much of school was like that—more a feeling than anything of substance.

"What's my part in all this?" I asked Hugh.

He led me away from the crowd thundering onto the metal bleachers and into a low hut marked LOCKER ROOMS. We slipped through a door that said VISITORS.

Hugh plucked a set of large pads off a wall hook

and placed them on my shoulders. "You're going to be out there with the team."

I was alarmed. "I don't know how to do football."

"Don't worry," he soothed me. "It isn't a game. You just have to show your support for the team."

As if on cue, the PA system crackled to life. "Faculty and students, give it up for your very own Claverage Condors!"

Running feet clattered in the hall outside. The field exploded with cheers. Even more deafening was the metallic boom of thousands of feet on the bleachers. A band was playing, but it was barely audible over the crowd noise.

"Am I late?" I asked anxiously.

"No," Hugh replied, "you're going to be right on time." He eased a yellow football jersey over my head and began tucking my hair under a matching helmet.

"Maybe I need a bigger hat," I suggested.

"Maybe you need a haircut," he countered, cramming the bulky headgear into place.

A faceguard lowered itself into my field of vision. I felt like I was peering out from behind a fence.

"Is that really necessary?" I asked.

"Definitely."

For an instant, I thought he looked kind of sad. I was concerned. "Is everything okay?"

"When is everything ever okay with me?" he complained. "Now get out there and make the school proud." He pointed me through the doorway, which led down a concrete tunnel and onto the field.

The crowd noise swelled to a deafening crescendo. But you know how cheers sound friendly? This was different—angrier. Mean, even. I scanned the bleachers and saw a sea of hostile faces staring straight at me

But I was here to support our team. I started walking toward the players just as they started toward me—and began to pick up speed. I could feel the ground shake as they reached a full-on stampede.

It was then that I made a startling discovery. They were all dressed in football uniforms like I was, but their jerseys were blue and red, not yellow like mine. I peered down at my chest and read, upside down, a single word: RHINECLIFF.

Why was I dressed as the other team?

21

NAME: **DARRYL PENNYFIELD**

The Rhinecliff game always cranked school spirit up to fever pitch, and the pep rally proved it. When that guy in the Rhinecliff jersey stepped onto the turf, the whole place went nuts. Sure, we understood that it wasn't a real Rhinecliff Raider who had wandered into our stadium. But every single player knew exactly what was supposed to come next.

By the time Zach yelled, "Get him!" most of us were already up to full speed.

I wasn't the fastest guy on the Condors. But I was the best tackler, and I was determined to get there first. I let the roar of the crowd fill me like rocket fuel, powering me past my teammates.

I swear—it never once crossed my mind to wonder who this kid was, this hero who was ready to be plowed down by the entire squad just to put on a good show. Whoever it was, it had to be a good athlete who could take a big hit.

The instant I made contact, I realized I was dead wrong. It was like tackling a punter. No, a punter's little sister. It was the worst feeling I ever had.

I tried to roll off, screaming at the others, "Stop!"

Too late. They were already airborne, coming in like a wave of guided missiles. I can't even describe the crunch. It wasn't pleasant for me either, because I was at the bottom. I can only imagine how it must have been for a skinny nonathlete who had no business setting foot on a gridiron. A bomb blast, an earthquake.

The crowd was in a frenzy, howling every time another Condor piled on.

Suddenly, the coaches were there, reaching into the tangle of arms and legs, pulling off bodies and tossing them aside. I heard Coach Pulaski bellowing, "What's the matter with you people? What was that all about?"

I jumped up and stared at him. "Wait a minute! That wasn't planned?"

The coach didn't answer. He was too busy getting the helmet off the guy in the Rhinecliff jersey.

About thirty pounds of hair spilled out onto the turf. Eleven hundred screaming, cheering kids went suddenly silent at the sight of the eighth grade president stretched out, dazed, on the grass.

I dropped to my knees beside him. "Cap, are you okay?"

Cap reached up and brushed at a clump of mud that had penetrated his faceguard. He started to say something, but it came out a low gurgle.

The coach and one of the trainers hauled Cap to his feet. Supporting him, one on each side, they began walking him back to the school building and the nurse's office. There was a smattering of applause like they give injured players at sporting events. But not much. Everybody was too shocked.

Before leaving the field, Coach Pulaski turned back to the team. "Nobody moves. Not a muscle. You hear me?"

They hustled Cap away. He was taking the occasional step, but if they hadn't been holding him up, he would have been flat on his face for sure.

Still silent, the crowd began to file out in an orderly fashion. They fell in line behind Cap and the coaches, like mourners in a funeral procession. There was none of the rowdiness and high spirits from before. Cap's injury had sucked all the pep out of this rally.

I looked at my teammates, moving from face to face, not sure if I was upset or just confused. "What happened? Why was Cap in that uniform?"

"I guess he volunteered," offered our kicker.

"Volunteered for what? That wasn't supposed to be part of the rally. The coaches knew nothing about it."

"Maybe Cap did the whole thing on his own," suggested Zach. "He's a bit of a nut job. Even you have to admit he's not Joe Average."

That should have been enough for me. It always had been before. The word of Zach Powers. He was the guy who convinced me I wasn't as stupid as I think I probably am. Before Zach, school was pure torture for me. Imagine spending 180 days a year in a place that's designed to take everything you're not good at and make it important. Zach rewrote those rules for me. School had nothing to do with learning and knowing and getting the right answers.

School was about sports and girls and fun and being popular, because you're good at sports, hang out with the right girls, and have a lot of fun.

But Zach had gotten so weird lately on the subject of Cap, how could I trust what he was saying? There was something about this disaster that just didn't add up.

I was still chewing on it when Coach Pulaski burst back upon us, his face a thundercloud.

"If there's one thing I tried to teach you besides the fundamentals of football, it's to use your head for something more than a place to put your helmet! What in God's name were you thinking?"

"Honest, Coach," protested one of the receivers. "We didn't know it was Cap."

Pulaski's eyes bulged. "But you knew it was *somebody*! Why would you think it's *ever* okay for twenty guys to pile on some poor kid like he's a tackling dummy? And not just for *his* sake! What about your own? You risk your bones, your knees, any chance of playing in high school—and for what? To beat up on a jersey that once belonged to Rhinecliff?"

"Is Cap going to be okay?" I asked in a small voice.

"Probably—no thanks to you. For crying out

loud, Pennyfield, I haven't seen you run that hard all season! Now, I've got to ask you—all of you: who put that boy up to playing kamikaze?"

I studied my cleats, and everybody else studied theirs.

"Come on," prodded the coach. "Somebody had to know about this." Again, dead silence. "Fine, don't tell me. But this isn't over. When Mr. Kasigi gets back, he's going to ask you these same questions and probably a lot more. I'm disgusted with every last one of you!"

We changed and went back to class, but there was no escaping the events of the pep rally. The whole school had been there to see what happened, and no one could talk about anything else. What went wrong? What did the team know, and when did they know it? Was Cap going to be all right?

The speculation got wilder every minute. One rumor actually had it that Cap might take revenge on the team by running us over with a school bus.

"Come on!" I exploded. "There's no revenge! It was an accident!"

Naomi was beyond furious. "Oh, sure, twenty guys *accidentally* jumped on him."

"Okay, that part was on purpose," I admitted. "But we didn't mean for it to be Cap. We didn't mean for it to be *anybody*. It was a stunt—like the guy in the jersey was Rhinecliff."

"Some stunt," she snapped. "Cap has never played football. You could have put him in the hospital!"

"Calm down," soothed Lena. "He isn't in any hospital. The word is he's still at school, and he's going to his afternoon classes. Limping a little, but not really hurt."

When Lena used the phrase "the word is," you could take it to the bank. She knew *everybody*. It was like she had her own private network of spies.

I heaved a sigh of relief. I'd been the first to hit Cap, after all. The shame brought sudden tears to my eyes.

Lena stuck her finger in my face. "Don't you dare start blubbering on me. None of this was your fault. It was Winkleman."

I was blown away. "*Hugh* Winkleman?"

"Phil saw him in the office getting bawled out for it."

None of us were Winkleman fans, but I couldn't believe Hugh would do anything to hurt Cap. Cap was the closest thing he had to a friend. Not to mention that the wuss didn't have the guts to hurt a fly—not unless someone else was pulling his strings.

I had a haunting vision from lunch yesterday. Hugh at a corner table, deep in conversation with Zach. Those two were worst enemies. Yet they had been hunched over that table almost like they were—plotting something?

Zach was the captain of the Condors. He knew about the pep rally. He knew the locker room setup and the longtime rivalry with Rhinecliff. And he had a grudge against Cap that was growing bigger every minute. . . .

I guess I must have looked like the Incredible Hulk—sickly green and bursting out of my shirt in sheer rage. My own best friend, the guy I admired so much that I tried to be just like him—

"Darryl, what's wrong?" Lena asked in alarm.

Without answering, I raced down the hall toward Zach's locker, each stride longer than the last. How many times had I gone there to be his sidekick and his yes-man, to tell him what he wanted to hear? Well, he wasn't going to want to hear this!

It was class change, so the corridor was crowded. I kept on moving. There was no point being a linebacker if you couldn't clear a path with your shoulder.

If I'd doubted Zach's guilt, the expression on his face when he saw me gave it all away. He knew I knew.

"*You!*" I accused. "You did that to Cap! You couldn't fight your own battles! You had to use the whole football team as a weapon!"

He played dumb. "What are you babbling about? I didn't do anything to Cap. It was Winkleman! Haven't you heard? It's all over the school."

"And who put him up to it?" I ranted. "I know it's you! I saw you two planning it in the cafeteria!"

"You're delusional!" It was classic Zach—the sneering, superior put-down tone that he used on other people, but never on me. "You're just feeling guilty because you're the one who hit him!"

"We *all* hit him!" I said hotly.

"But who got there first? You practically broke your neck doing it. No way were you going to be denied the pleasure of planting your helmet right between those numbers."

The fact that he was one hundred percent right

made me that much madder. I was so pumped with rage that I didn't notice Cap himself joining the spectators around us.

Zach wasn't done yet. "To be honest, I'm kind of impressed, Darryl. I never knew you could get that kind of speed out of that fat caboose of yours."

And I snapped. Totally. Zach was smarter than I was, and I was never going to win this argument using just my mouth. It was time for my knuckles to take over.

Honest—I didn't even know Cap was there. I didn't recognize the voice that said, "Violence is not the answer." All I felt was my fist slamming into something about eighteen inches closer than its intended receiver.

When the burning haze cleared from my eyes, the first person I saw was Zach, untouched and laughing at me. Down at my feet lay Cap, out cold, his nose gushing blood like a geyser.

"Not again! No!" I whimpered, horror-struck.

The hall just about exploded with agitated chatter. The news spread like wildfire that the eighth grade president was down again.

Zach was practically hysterical. "That's the second time today that you've decked this kid. You're building a great relationship. If you get any closer, you'll probably kill him!"

The reality of what I'd done overpowered even the desire to shut Zach's big mouth. I hauled Cap off the floor. "Help me!" I bawled at the crowd.

A couple of sixth graders rushed up to support Cap on the other side. We hustled him through the maze of gawkers. I noticed he was starting to come around, because he was mumbling about peace and nonviolence. His breathing blew pink bubbles in the torrent of blood that was still pouring from his nose.

I was so flustered that it never even occurred to me to lie when Nurse Myerson asked what happened.

"You were in a fight?" she demanded.

"Not with Cap! I was trying to punch someone else, but his face got in the way! It was all because of nonviolence!"

"I can see that," she said coldly.

But her attention was on Cap, so I got sent to wait for her in the principal's office. I sat there through the final period of the day, not even agonizing over what "I'll deal with you later" might mean. Whatever happened to me, I definitely had it coming.

The rest of the school seemed to think so too, because I got a lot of dirty looks as I stewed there in full view behind the glass. The condemned man on public display—the guy who had KOed Cap, and tackled him before that.

The worst part was that I liked Cap now. Sure, I'd been awful to him. But that had been back in the days when we'd made him president as a joke and sent him wandering after fake press conferences and stole his shoes while he was meditating. Back when Zach had been calling the shots. What a bunch of jerks we'd been, firing spitballs at a kid just because his hippie hair made a big target.

And in spite of everything we threw at him, Cap never fell apart, or ratted us out, or even got mad. For weeks it had been open season on the eighth grade president, but he hung in there. That's what first brought me around to admire the guy. I didn't care that he could drive a bus or plan a dance. Cap Anderson was *quality*.

I didn't see that before. I saw it now. Yet now was when I'd really hurt him.

I was never going to forgive myself.

The bell rang, but Nurse Myerson still hadn't appeared. The halls filled with students packing up for the day. Through the main doors, I could see the fleet of yellow buses coming up the circular drive. And there, between the third and fourth—

An ambulance.

No. It couldn't be. Not for Cap. There was no siren. It was driving normal speed, taking its turn in the queue. Still—what would an ambulance be doing in a line of school buses?

The answer rounded the corner ten feet in front of me. It was Nurse Myerson, escorting a shaky, blood-spattered Cap toward the front door. The crowd parted to let them through. Outside, kids waiting to board their buses formed an aisle that led to the rear of the EMS unit.

I didn't care how much trouble I was in. I raced out of the office and blasted through the double doors. The scene was eerie. All eyes were on Cap, but no one was saying a word—not a peep, not even a whisper. The only sounds were the idling engines and the flapping of the flag on the pole.

I cupped my hands to my mouth. "Cap, I'm sorry! It was an accident! Both times!"

I was too late. Nurse Myerson helped him up into the ambulance, and the greatest eighth grade president we ever had was gone.

22

NAME: **CAPRICORN ANDERSON**

The back doors of the ambulance swung open, and there she was.

She sat in a wheelchair that was anchored to the floor. She looked paler and thinner, but never better—not to me.

I hugged her. "Rain, I missed you so much."

She hugged me back, then pulled away and held me at arm's length. "I see that. Have you been in a fight?"

"I tried to stop one," I admitted. "I guess I've got a lot to learn about peacemaking."

She nodded proudly. "Good for you. We always try to save the world. But sometimes the world doesn't want to be saved." She looked at me critically. "You're going to have two black eyes, you know."

I grinned at her. "I'll take *four* black eyes if you tell me we're going back to Garland."

"We're going home, Cap. I think the rehab center was glad to get rid of me. Some of my opinions didn't sit well with my fellow patients. Like it's a crime to speak your mind." She beamed. "I insisted we come straight here to pick you up. I didn't want you to have to spend an extra minute in this awful place."

"It's not *so* bad," I told her. "Different. Crazy. But there are good things about it too."

"You're a kind soul," she praised me. "But it's all over now. We just have to stop at Floramundi's and pick up your things."

The EMS tech slammed the door and turned to Rain. "We've got to run the siren for a few seconds or we're not allowed to pass the school buses. Nothing to worry about."

The vehicle whooped and wailed off school property, then returned to making its silent way through traffic to the Donnellys'.

I ran into the house calling, "Mrs. Donnelly! Mrs. Donnelly!" I was anxious to share my good news with the lady who had been so nice to me.

Sophie looked up from the depths of a Department of Motor Vehicles pamphlet entitled *Welcome New Driver*. "She's at work, just like every other day. What's so important?"

"I'm leaving," I told her.

"Don't let the door slap you in the butt on the way out," she said, stifling a yawn. "When will you be back?"

"Never," I replied. "Rain picked me up straight from the hospital. We're going home."

She put down the manual. "No fooling." She peered out the kitchen window at the ambulance parked in the driveway. "Sweet ride. Your grandmother's in there?"

I nodded. "She can't come in. She's still not getting around so well. Do you want to go out and meet her?"

"That's okay," she said quickly. "My mother's been telling me Rain stories for years. I feel like I already know her." She took in my swollen face and blood-spattered tie-dye. "Whoa! You sure that ambulance isn't for you?"

I was embarrassed. "My nose started bleeding at school. I'm fine."

"You looked like you killed and ate a wild boar," she commented mildly. "Come on, I'll help you get your stuff together."

It took barely a few minutes to fill my duffel bag and erase the fact that I'd ever lived in this house. I'm not sure what made me ask if I could have the Claverage yearbooks. All that was behind me now. But studying them had become almost like a hobby.

"Knock yourself out," Sophie insisted. "You're doing us a favor by making that stuff disappear."

I wrote a note to Mrs. Donnelly, thanking her for letting me stay there. I could have ended up in some kind of group home for all those weeks. I made sure to tell her that Rain was grateful too, since they had known each other.

"I guess this is it, then," said Sophie.

I paused at the TV, the only one I might ever get to watch *Trigonometry and Tears* on. "I can't believe I'm never going to find out how Rishon does in college."

"Oh, he never makes it to college," she informed me. "He gets run over by a cement truck on the way to freshman orientation."

I was shattered. *"No!"*

She laughed. "I'm just pulling your chain. I'm sure he lives on to be a total basket case just like everybody else on *T & T*. He doesn't exist, remember? I'd say 'get a clue,' but where you're going, you're probably better off without one."

We exchanged a very awkward good-bye. I wished her luck with the driving test, and she told me to have a nice life. It gave me a special glow to note that she was wearing the bracelet she thought was a gift from her father.

"It was real, it was fun, but it wasn't real fun," she called as I headed down the front walk.

It seemed fitting that the last thing she said to me was something I didn't understand.

I got back into the ambulance and we drove off. I knew I'd never forget Sophie Donnelly.

"Next stop, Garland," Rain told me.

I couldn't keep myself from grinning, which made my nose hurt.

It was about an hour's drive. It would have taken even longer, but the driver used his siren to open up some snarled traffic.

I could tell the instant we turned onto the dirt road that led to the community. I had memorized every pothole and rut in that driveway, and they were all precious to me. The fact of returning hadn't become real until that moment.

The ambulance stopped, and the attendants helped us out and up onto our own porch. The first thing I noticed was that the duct tape had come off my Foucault pendulum. The bowling-ball weight had fallen, cracking the floorboards.

I took in the sights and smells of the only home I'd ever known up until several weeks ago. It looked smaller than I remembered it, and more—used. The colors and textures seemed very bland compared to the warm and bright bricks and stuccos of the houses around C Average.

I felt a pang of guilt for my disloyal thought. This was the greatest, most beloved spot on earth! If it looked a little run-down, it was from all the weeks standing empty.

Rain could always read my mind. "The place is lonely. It missed us."

Not half as much as I missed it.

23

NAME: **MR. KASIGI**

The conference could not possibly have gone better. I was congratulated by so many people that it was almost embarrassing. Our own district superintendent confided that the principalship of North High would be opening up in a couple of years, and the job was mine for the asking.

I felt fantastic. Why wouldn't I? I returned to Claverage flushed with victory. I had no way of knowing that the key word in that sentence was going to be "flushed."

I'd expected a huge pile of mail, and a lot of phone messages and e-mails. But as I sifted through the papers and envelopes on my desk, the familiar logo of the Consolidated Savings Bank kept turning up.

I opened the one marked "Urgent" and unfolded the computer-generated page inside.

> *Dear Customer,*
> *We are returning this check to you because your*
> *account is overdrawn and the transaction cannot be*
> *honored. A service fee of $30.00 has been charged to*
> *your account.*

Stapled to the page was a Claverage Middle School check with INSUFFICIENT FUNDS stamped across it in red. It was made out to the American Cancer Society in the amount of five hundred dollars. My own signature appeared on one of the lines. On the second was written *Capricorn Anderson.*

My office tilted, and I clung to the arms of my chair for fear of winding up on the carpet. This was one of the checks I'd given Anderson! Why was he donating five hundred dollars to the American Cancer Society? Not that it wasn't a worthy cause. But this money was supposed to pay for the Halloween dance!

Hands shaking, I opened a few more envelopes. They were all the same—the March of Dimes, Habitat for Humanity, Cystic Fibrosis Foundation, all for hundreds.

An icy feeling spread northward from the base of my spine. If these checks were bouncing, it meant the money in the Student Activities Fund was *gone*! There had been four thousand dollars in that account!

I waded into the mountain of mail with both hands, tossing envelopes in all directions, until I came up with the bank statement. On it, the whole terrible story was laid out for me in detail.

There were the checks that I'd countersigned, the ones that had bounced, and the ones that hadn't. I saw the deposits for the food and music, and one or two other expenses that probably had to do with the dance. The rest were all made out to charities. One, to the March of Caring, was for a thousand dollars!

What was going on here?

I buzzed my secretary. "Get Capricorn Anderson down to my office. Immediately!"

"Capricorn Anderson is no longer a registered student here."

I nearly inhaled my tie. "Since when?"

"He left the school last Wednesday," came the reply. "His grandmother was released from the hospital."

"Get her on the phone!"

There was a brief pause, then, "It says here they don't have a phone."

I did the only thing I could think of. I called Flora Donnelly. I left messages at her home, office, and cell number. I must have sounded pretty desperate, because she turned up within the hour.

By that time, I had already spoken to my bank manager and a very unfriendly assistant to the deejay, who accused me of ". . . hangin' rubber paper offa my man, yo," whatever that meant.

I turned beseeching eyes to the social worker. "This is your case, Flora. I know you have a special connection to the kid. Can you shine any light on this for me?"

She examined the evidence—the bank statements and the bounced checks. Her face was a sickly shade of gray. She looked like I felt.

Then she said something I didn't expect: "Frank, this is all your fault."

"*My* fault?"

"What possessed you to give him signed checks?"

"I was going out of town!" I defended myself. "I didn't want him to be caught short. Besides, we always give the kids some responsibility with the Student Activity Fund. They're teenagers. They're supposed to be able to handle it."

"I warned you that Cap Anderson is a boy who may as well have been raised on another planet."

"Okay," I admitted, "I noticed he wasn't exactly streetwise. But that didn't stop him from committing fraud."

"He's no more capable of fraud than of flying," she said flatly.

"It's right there in black and white!" I insisted. "He found a way to take the school's money and make it look like he donated it to charity. I've got no choice but to call the police."

She was suddenly patient. "When you gave him those checks, did you explain to him what a check is and how it works?"

"Of course. I'm not a fool."

"No," she said. "I mean *exactly* how it works. That the amount of the check is deducted from the balance in the account? And that the money can run out?"

"Everybody knows you can't spend more than you have!"

"Frank, I never told you this. I lived on Garland Farm until I was twelve. When my family moved, I had never handled money. Not even a penny. Money was the key to everything that was wrong with the world, and the leaders of the community kept any kind of financial dealings completely hidden from us kids. I *guarantee* you that Cap had no idea that anyone had to pay for the checks he was writing. And the power to write them must have seemed almost magical. Once he realized that he could use that power to help people, there was no limit to how much he might try to give away."

I was thunderstruck. "Are you telling me that he really *did* take the entire Student Activity Fund and donate it to charity?"

She nodded. "He's got all the idealism of the sixties with none of the reality checks. He's not a criminal, he's the exact opposite—totally innocent in every sense of the word."

I held my head. "It would have been easier if he'd robbed the school at gunpoint and taken off for the Mexican border. *That* I could have explained to the board, and insurance would have covered it. What am I going to do? Call the March of Dimes and demand my money back?"

"You could try," she suggested reasonably. "This can't be the first time an unauthorized person misspent money."

"Yeah, to buy a plasma TV, not to donate to charity."

Her face betrayed a ghost of a smile. "Don't worry. At Garland there's nowhere to plug in a plasma TV."

"Here's a charge that doesn't look very charitable," I muttered, still studying the bank statement. "It's to a jewelry store on Main Street."

She looked over my shoulder. "I'm sure there's some explanation. Prizes, probably. Best dancer, best rap, most outrageous outfit—that kind of thing."

I nodded numbly. That was the moment when I realized there would be no dancing prizes, because there would be no dance.

It wouldn't be a popular decision, but I saw now that this was the only way. Sure, I could fight with the bank, or plead with the charities. But it would just make me look like a fool. Or I could drive out to this Garland place and demand that the grandmother replace the funds Cap frittered away. Still—who knew if they had any money at all? They were living an alternative lifestyle forty years after the rest of the world had given it up. The local papers would have a field day reporting that while I was running a principals' conference in Las Vegas, my trusted eighth grade president was emptying my treasury.

The job at North High was not going to be offered to a court jester.

No, I had to cancel the dance, recoup what I could, and eat the rest.

Flora Donnelly was right. This *was* my fault. But not for her reasons. I had long suspected how the kids went about picking their eighth grade president. And when I chose to look the other way, I was sort of putting a stamp of approval on it. But I always knew that one day it would blow up in their faces.

I just never thought it would blow up in mine.

24

NAME: **NAOMI ERLANGER**

What were we supposed to think?

First Cap gets crushed by the entire football team, and the coaches practically have to carry him to the nurse. Three hours later, he gets decked by Darryl Pennyfield—I'm never speaking to *him* again. Next thing you know, he's being taken away by ambulance.

I hadn't seen him since.

Okay, for the first couple of days, nobody was surprised Cap was absent from school. He was hurting. Who wouldn't be? Then the weekend— the Condors game on Saturday. Well, who could blame him for blowing off that event after what the team did to him? Lena only went because she's a cheerleader, and she said it was the lousiest turnout she'd ever seen for a Condors-Raiders matchup. (C Average and Rhinecliff battled to a 3-3 tie, in case you're one of the few who cares.)

Serves those jerks right.

Anyway, I figured I'd catch Cap on Monday. Wrong. And by Tuesday, I was getting worried. It was almost a full week since anybody had laid eyes on the eighth grade president.

Okay, I was extra upset because Cap was extra special to me. But everyone was talking about it. You'd see a bunch of kids in a huddle in the hall, and you didn't have to eavesdrop to figure out the topic of conversation. Where was Cap? Why hadn't he come back yet? Could he be really hurt? The custodians were still trying to scrub his blood off the terrazzo in the corridor where the big punch had been thrown.

He must have been in bad shape. What else would keep him away from what was brewing between the two of us? "To be continued"—I *meant* that. This wasn't another shallow middle school crush like the one I'd had on Zach. This was a *relationship*. And besides, the Halloween dance was on

Saturday night. Cap had to realize we could never pull it off without him.

When I asked Mrs. Vogel, my homeroom teacher, she replied, "I don't think Cap Anderson is a student here anymore."

"What?" She might as well have told me that the school was slated for demolition with all of us inside it. "Of course he's a student! He's the eighth grade president!"

She looked uncomfortable. "I don't want to argue with you, Naomi. I've told you what I know."

"I'm going to ask Mr. Kasigi!" I stormed.

"Who do you think told me?" she said, not unkindly. "Mr. Kasigi held an emergency staff meeting to bring all the teachers up to speed. I don't recommend that you mention Cap's name to him. He gets very emotional on the subject."

"But the dance is Saturday night! Who's going to run it if Cap isn't here?"

She wouldn't look me in the eye. "The announcement is going to be made at lunch. The dance has been canceled."

I felt like I'd been hit in the stomach with a two-by-four. "You can't be serious!"

She was serious enough to kick me out of the

room. By the time I staggered into the hall, the first of the notices was being posted:

**DUE TO UNFORTUNATE CIRCUMSTANCES,
THE HALLOWEEN DANCE HAS BEEN
CALLED OFF.**

As you can imagine, the chaos was rising. There was only one middle school in Claverage. Our neighbors had all gone here; our older brothers and sisters. A lot of our parents had attended C Average. There had *always* been a Halloween dance.

"They can't cancel the dance!" wailed Tiffany Peterson. "It's a tradition!"

"They can and they did," Lena said darkly. "Kasigi's such a jerk. He spends the week partying at some fancy convention, and then comes home to pull the plug on anybody else having fun."

"But it's our trademark!" Tiffany persisted. "The elementaries have holiday pageants; the high school has Homecoming. Halloween is *our thing*! How can Mr. Kasigi do this to us?"

Zach put his two cents in. "Kasigi isn't the problem. Since when do the teachers have much to say about what goes on in this place? You're ignoring the obvious: the dance got canceled because Cap screwed up somehow."

"How do you figure that?" asked Lena. "The details are all set, and Cap isn't even here."

"Exactly," Zach agree. "It's *his* party. Where is he?"

I jumped on that so fast, the wind should have knocked him over. "Where is he? It was your precious football team that tried to put him through the crust of the earth. And don't forget the punch that leveled him was meant for you."

He shrugged. "It's not my fault Pennyfield's gone over the edge."

"Nothing's ever your fault," I snarled at him. "When you couldn't use Cap as your clown, you tried to use him as your crash-test dummy. I've had it up to here with you, Zach Powers! You and I are *through*!"

As rattled as I was, I took some satisfaction in the expression of total shock on his face. I laid it on even thicker. "Did it ever occur to you that 'unfortunate circumstances' might not be just a lame excuse? What if it means—what if it means—"

Well, what *could* it mean? No one had the guts to say it, but it was in everybody's thoughts. Stone-faced Mr. Kasigi couldn't hear Cap's name because it made him too emotional. What unfortunate circumstances could cause that? Add in the fact that Cap had dropped off the face of the earth. . . .

"Let's get to the bottom of this," Lena decided.

Good old Lena. She was a tough nut, but she could be so sensible sometimes. Plus, she had tons of connections, and everybody seemed to owe her a favor. Phil Ruiz helped out around the office, so Lena made it his job to get into student records and pull Cap's file.

He snuck the folder out in the kangaroo pocket of his hooded sweatshirt and showed it to us in the stairwell by the gym.

This is what it contained: nothing. No papers, no grades, no test scores, not so much as an index card.

"How is it possible to have an empty file?" Lena demanded.

"It isn't," Phil told her. "It should have transcripts, transfer forms from his old school, and emergency contact information."

"That's what we need!" I exploded. "We have to contact him. This is an emergency!"

"Don't worry," Lena said darkly. "Somebody must have his address."

I rode the same bus as Cap, but my stop was before his, so I had no idea where he got off. We couldn't find anyone who knew which house was his.

Then, at last, a breakthrough. Olivia Weintraub had a brother who had once dated a girl named Sophie Donnelly. He had talked about a longhaired sixties-type staying with the Donnellys. It could only have been Cap.

Lena and I took Cap's bus after school and found the right house, a well-kept split level on a quiet side street. Just the thought that he lived and slept here made me feel warm inside. I was positive we had the right place.

"This is it," Lena confirmed. "191 Rockcrest."

As we marched up the walk to the front door, the window of a car parked in the driveway whispered open. A very pretty high school girl leaned out and called, "Something I can do for you?"

"Does Cap Anderson live here?" I asked anxiously.

"No." She started to roll the window up again.

The passenger door opened and an older lady got out. "You girls are too late. Cap is—no longer at this address."

You could hear she was choosing her words carefully.

"Well," Lena persisted, "can you tell us where he is now?"

"I'm afraid that's not possible."

"But why?" I wailed. "We really need to talk to him!"

The daughter lowered her window again. "My driving test is the day after tomorrow. We're busy."

"Sorry, girls," the mother added. "I'm sure you're just friends, with the best of intentions. But a lot of things have happened that I'm not at liberty to talk about." She got back inside and shut the door.

"Can't you just give us his phone number?" I begged.

The teenager gave me an odd smile. "Where he is they don't have a phone."

They drove away, leaving us standing on their doorstep, stunned.

Finally, Lena spoke, her voice subdued. "I think I might know why we can't find Cap."

Meltdown—that's the only word to describe my state of mind. For months I had been wandering the desert, throwing myself at that undeserving creep Zach. Now—*finally*—I understood my true feelings.

And it was too late.

Up until that moment, no one had dared to speak the awful words out loud. But I couldn't keep them bottled inside me any longer.

"What if he's dead?"

25

NAME: **ZACH POWERS**

First things first: I didn't believe it for a heartbeat.

The rumors were beyond nuts. Cap's in the hospital . . . He's in the morgue . . . He's in a persistent vegetative state . . . He's suffering from amnesia . . . He's upside down in a fish tank. . . .

I'd lost all respect for the intelligence level in this place. They should raffle off the Brooklyn Bridge at the next PTA fund-raiser.

I couldn't explain where Cap was, and frankly, I didn't care. Not only was my year in ruins, but my name was mud at C Average. Me—Zach Powers! And it was all thanks to the Case of the Disappearing Hairball.

People were nuts on the subject. I don't think I heard a single conversation on any other topic. Teachers were complaining that their students could focus on nothing else. I figured most of the kids were just bummed that the dance had been canceled. No—people were genuinely worried about the hippie!

"What's the big deal?" I said for the umpteenth time. "So he slipped back through the same time warp he dropped out of in the first place."

Naomi cut me dead with a flamethrower glare. "You never liked him! You tried to make a fool of him!"

It was scary how much that girl hated me now. I used to think she was kind of hot for me. Maybe I misread the signs.

"Yeah," I admitted. "So did you. So did the whole eighth grade."

"But then *some of us* saw the kind of person Cap was," Lena put in. "*Some of us* appreciate how he devoted his heart and soul to the school."

"Heart and soul?" I exploded. "He held a funeral for a bird! He danced on the front lawn! He played senior citizen music! The Beatles and that other grandpa—Guitarfunkel, or whatever his name is."

"Garfunkel," Naomi corrected icily. "Simon and Garfunkel."

"Listen," Lena told me, "Cap gave his *life*—"

"He *didn't*—"

But I was fighting a losing battle. If Lena believed it, it might as well have been the lead story on CNN. Cap put his all into C Average, and for that he was struck down. If he wasn't dead, he was seriously messed up.

"Just because you can't find someone doesn't mean he's at death's door!" I argued with at least twenty people. "I can't tell you exactly where Tom Cruise is, either. That doesn't make him a corpse."

Talk to the wall. Eleven hundred kids were absolutely convinced that the eighth grade president had come to tragedy. And it was all thanks to the football team, Darryl Pennyfield, and me.

I couldn't take three steps in the hall without getting a dirty look from somebody. Even sixth graders felt they had the right to scowl in my direction. Every time I came back to my locker there was a fresh insult scratched into the paint: *jerk*, *dope*, or something else with the same number of letters.

"Has everybody gone off the deep end?" I complained to Hugh in the cafeteria. "When the Garrets redid their kitchen, nobody saw Alicia for like, three weeks. Not one person thought she was dead."

"Yeah, but the whole school didn't watch Alicia Garret being loaded into an ambulance," he pointed out. "And the biggest party of the year wasn't canceled right after that."

I scowled at him. "Don't tell me you're about to join the chorus of mourners for our dear departed Sasquatch."

"Of course not," he told me. "I think it's a load of hooey. But I can't say I'm surprised. If this school was full of geniuses, I'd have a lot more company on the chess team."

It was the ultimate barometer of my plummeting status. The only person willing to eat lunch with me was Hugh. If I could track Cap down using hippie LoJack, I wouldn't know whether to haul him back or hide out with him. Part of me just wanted to disappear.

"Hey, what's that?" Suddenly, Hugh reached over and began rifling through my hair.

I slapped his arm away. "Cut it out, man!"

"Look!" He plucked a small object from behind my ear and held it in front of me—a pea-size blob of soggy white paper.

A spitball.

I examined it, unbelieving. "That's impossible—"

He was disgusted. "Spitballs can travel both ways, you know. You don't have a force field around you."

I stared at him, the target of more of my spitballs than everybody else put together. "I suppose you're waiting for an apology."

"I'm just enjoying my front row seat at Payback Fest," he sneered.

"Hey, you bring a lot of it on yourself," I accused.

"It's *my* fault I get picked on?"

"From the first day of kindergarten, everything about you screamed *dweeb*—your clothes, your hobbies, your vocabulary—"

He scowled. "And you're perfect."

I told the truth. "My whole life, it's always been obvious what sports to play, what bands to listen to, what people to hang out with. It's as if I was born with a natural guidance system inside my head, showing me how to be cool." My brow clouded. "But Cap Anderson doesn't come with a book of instructions."

Instead of gloating, he actually seemed to understand. For Hugh Winkleman, the whole planet didn't come with a book of instructions.

He said, "Too bad you can't just start liking him."

If he had smacked me with a brick, I couldn't have been any more stunned. How could I have missed something so obvious? "Hugh, that's it!" I exclaimed. "If we can't stop this hippie bandwagon, we'll have to find a way to jump on."

"Isn't it a little too late for that?" he challenged. "Cap may not be dead, but he's definitely gone."

"We might be able to work that to our advantage. Come on."

I strode out of the lunchroom and across the hall to the library. He wolfed down what was left of his sandwich and followed.

I logged on to a computer, pounded the keyboard for a few moments, and swiveled the screen toward him. His eyes widened as he read:

A TRIBUTE TO CAP ANDERSON

PAY YOUR RESPECTS TO
THE BEST 8TH GRADE PRESIDENT EVER
SATURDAY, 7 P.M.
(THE TIME OF THE HALLOWEEN DANCE
HE NEVER GOT TO GIVE US)
IN THE PARKING LOT

DO *NOT* SHOW TO ANY TEACHERS!

He tried to say something, and began to choke on a mouthful of peanut butter and jelly.

I pounded him on the back, cackling with glee. Zach Powers was down but not out!

"Load the paper tray. We've got a lot of printing to do."

26

NAME: **SOPHIE DONNELLY**

T-day at last. My driving test.

Things were finally falling into place. Dad had come through with the bracelet. I was an only child again. Life was even looking up on the boyfriend front—for the last couple of days I'd been on the receiving end of some intense glances from Martin Enfield, a senior on the lacrosse team.

Now I just had to pass this test. Dad phoned to wish me luck, going on and on about how proud he was. He talked as if he'd been my mentor and not someone who'd finally showed up to give me a few lessons before blowing town. But it was good to hear his voice. And anyway, I had something to say to him on a previous topic.

"Thanks for getting the bracelet back to me. The inscription—it was really sweet."

There was dead silence on the other end of the line.

"Dad, are you there?"

"Yeah, Soph, I'm here," the reply came at last. "I'm on my cell, and the connection isn't great. What was that about the bracelet?"

"Just thank you. The inscription—I never knew you were so sentimental."

"Glad your old man can still get the job done," he said smoothly. "Listen, Soph, you're breaking up. I can barely hear you. Good luck on the test. Knock 'em dead—"

The line went silent.

I hung up, frowning. The connection hadn't seemed so terrible to me. Even more confusing was his reaction to my thank-you for the bracelet. For a moment there I could have sworn he didn't have the faintest idea what I was talking about.

My mother bustled in: "Ready to go?"

"Mother, do you think Dad could have already forgotten about sending back the engraved bangle?"

She gave me that sympathetic social-worker look that she normally reserved for her loser clients like Cap Anderson. "Your father loves you, and he always has the best of intentions."

Ask a simple question, get a load of touchy-feely psychobabble in return. "So I should take that as a yes?"

"Honey, this is such a big day for you. Why would you dwell on something that's only going to make you unhappy?"

Whatever.

The waiting room at the DMV was decorated with large, mounted photographs of multivehicle pileups. Real subtle. Truth be told, I was scared to death. When the examiner got into the car, I honestly thought I might lose my lunch.

"Make a left out of the parking lot," he instructed.

It was a wet day—not pouring rain, but misty. That spooked me too. Turning the wheel, working the pedals—these things should have been second nature. Today they seemed awkward and complicated, like I was defusing a bomb. One wrong move and—*boom*.

To calm my nerves I tried to replace the

instructor with a mental image of Dad in the passenger seat. Yet, for some reason, the imaginary companion my brain conjured up was not my father, but Cap. I shook my head to reboot, but he was still there. The freakazoid was coming with me on the most important test of my life!

And why did the examiner have to take me down such a narrow street? There were parked cars on both sides, with very little road between them. Oh, no—

I was on the edge of panic when a familiar voice sounded inside my skull: *If the front gets through, the rest will drag.*

Gritting my teeth, I aimed the hood into the tight passage and held on for dear life. It was all I could do to keep from cheering as the Saturn threaded the needle.

Thanks, Cap. It was a good thing Rain drove a taxi before devoting her life to terrorizing my mother.

"Turn on to the interstate," the examiner ordered.

I took it slow merging onto the highway. As we picked up speed, droplets of water began running down the windshield. I set the wipers on intermittent, feeling a little more confident.

Still, my mind kept returning to the phone conversation with Dad. Believe me, I knew the man was a flake. But how could he forget about the bracelet? He didn't just give it to me—he presented it, took it away, had it engraved, and then brought it to the post office to mail. Anything with that many steps would stick in your mind, wouldn't it?

"Exit here and head east on Fillmore . . ."

I obsessed on the subject until the bangle on my wrist felt like an iron shackle from some medieval dungeon. How I managed to operate the car was a total mystery. I was completely distracted. And the more I twisted the facts, the more they pointed to a single inescapable conclusion.

Dad didn't *forget* about the engraved bracelet. He never sent it to me in the first place. It must have been Mother.

That wasn't her style, though. Not that she wanted me to be miserable. But the one thing she always said about her job was, "I can't let these kids live in a fantasy land." She was always nagging people to face reality, even me. *Especially* me, when the subject was my father.

It made no sense that she'd go through an

elaborate ruse to trick me into believing that he'd followed through on his promise.

But if not her, then who?

". . . and I just need you to parallel park between these orange cones," the examiner was saying. "Run the defogger a minute to make sure you can see out the back."

I reached for the button and missed. Instead, my finger hit the *on* switch for the radio. Music filled the car—the Beatles singing the chorus of "All You Need Is Love."

"Anyone who lived through the sixties will remember this old classic," came the deejay's voice as the song began its slow fade.

And suddenly, there were tears streaming down my cheeks.

The examiner was appalled. "There's no need to cry, miss! It's no big deal—you just hit the wrong button. I won't take off any points for that!"

"No, it's not that—" I managed, still blubbering. But how could I ever explain it? The radio! The *song*!

That engraved bangle wasn't from Dad *or* Mother! All You Need Is Love? There was only one person who could have come up with that inscription.

Cap.

I crunched all four orange cones. The examiner passed me anyway. I think he just felt sorry for me.

At that point, I was so broken up I don't think I would have noticed if the car had burst into flames. Cap had bought the bracelet and had it engraved just so I wouldn't feel bad about Dad blowing me off. He got absolutely nothing in return. He wasn't my boyfriend; he wasn't even my friend. He couldn't expect so much as a thank-you, since the gift was supposed to be from someone else. He did this for no other reason than to make me happy.

When I got back to the waiting room, Mother took one look at my red eyes and ashen complexion and assumed the worst.

"Never mind, honey. You'll take the test again."

I lashed out at her. "Get a clue, Mother! I have to go pick up my license."

She was astonished. "Then why are you crying?"

Why? Because I had never said a civil word to Capricorn Anderson. From the day he'd first set foot in our house, I'd declared war on the poor kid. I'd called him freakazoid, poured water on him, and never missed a chance to point out what a loser he was.

And he'd responded by doing the most wonderful thing anyone had ever done for me.

I clamped my jaw shut. The last thing I wanted was to let this slip in front of my mother. I felt horrible enough as it was.

I couldn't even enjoy the moment of being a licensed driver—almost as if it was unfair for something good to happen to a rotten person like me.

And the worst part was it was too late for me ever to make it up to Cap. He was gone, sucked back into 1967. His last chance at having a life was shot.

I thought back to myself in eighth grade—all the good times still to come. But not for him. He was buried in his ponchos and peace signs.

Tomorrow was Halloween. Those Halloween dances were the best thing about middle school. The poor guy got hauled off to the freak farm before he even had a chance to party, get wild, actually dance with a girl.

And there was nothing anybody could do about it.

Unless . . .

27

NAME: **CAPRICORN ANDERSON**

I gave the picking pole an expert twist. When I felt the weight of the apple in the canvas catcher, I lowered it to deposit yet another McIntosh into the basket. It was overripe and not as firm as it should be.

Everything at Garland was like that—neglected. And with Rain still hobbling around on a cane, most of the extra work was falling on me.

On the whole, we'd been lucky. The fruit was a little past its prime, but the potatoes, carrots, and turnips were in good shape.

The really great news was that Rain was making a full recovery. Just being at Garland seemed to energize her. By the second day home, she was driving again, taking our truck into town to restock our supplies. She didn't even need me to go with her.

"There's plenty to be done right here," she told me. "Besides, I think you've had enough of civilization for a while."

I got her point. I had two black eyes, and my nose still hurt where Darryl had punched it. A wounded raccoon—that's how Rain described me.

So off she went, leaving me filling the root cellar with bushel baskets of vegetables, pruning the fruit trees, spreading the compost—getting ready for winter.

It was Garland—my Garland—everything I'd longed for all these weeks. And I was happy to be home.

But . . .

My mind kept wandering back to the halls of C Average Middle School—the crash of locker doors, the babble of excited conversation. The ringing of cell phones, the beeping of Game Boys, the traces of far-off rap music escaping the ear buds of a hundred iPods.

It was crowded, noisy, obnoxious, and even scary. But it had its own rhythm and urgency and life. And

I missed it so much it was almost like an ache.

At night I spent hours poring over the year-books. Each familiar face triggered an avalanche of memories: tai chi on the lawn, singalongs in the music room, tie-dying, the hundreds upon hundreds of Halloween dance volunteers.

I looked around Garland, and in my heart, I knew it was the best place for me. But the quiet, the dull beiges and greens, the familiar farm chores, the complete lack of other people—this used to be my life; it used to be enough. Before.

Did I want to go back? How could I? I spent all my time *there* wishing I was *here*. Yet that life kept calling me. I wanted to eat food that was scooped onto my tray by crabby ladies in hairnets and greasy aprons. I wanted to watch reruns of *Trigonometry and Tears*. I wanted to twist the little metal dial to those mysterious numbers that would magically open my locker. I wanted Sophie Donnelly to call me freakazoid one more time.

In just a couple of hours, the Halloween dance would be starting. It was the responsibility of the eighth grade president. Okay, I knew nothing about dances and had planned zero percent of this one. But I should be there.

I'd asked Rain just that morning if I could go, and she'd said no.

"All that's behind you now, Cap. Our life is here."

"I know that," I told her. "But my name is on all the posters. How can I let everybody down?"

"They won't even notice you're not there," she assured me. "You know how people are in the outside world. Only interested in themselves and their own mindless fun."

I tried another argument. "But you always said we should finish what we start, see things through to the end—"

"Cap, when you left that school, that *was* the end. And a good thing too. You were only there for a couple of months, and see how much you've changed: you talk about television programs and waste your time staring at silly yearbooks. Thank goodness I was able to take you away before the contamination got any worse."

Contamination. That was the word she kept using. Like I'd spent her recovery wallowing in a toxic waste dump. Sure, the Donnelly house and C Average weren't much like the life Rain and I had built at Garland. But different didn't automatically mean bad.

Yet the more I talked about my experiences of the past eight weeks, the more upset she got. Not angry—that would be a sign of spiritual imbalance. Just really, really *worried*.

Maybe she was right. I *was* contaminated. Would I ever have stood up to her before my time away from Garland?

And for sure I never would have done what I was about to do.

I tore a small piece from the duct tape roll and fastened the note to our refrigerator.

DEAR RAIN,
I'M SORRY, BUT THIS IS JUST TOO
IMPORTANT. DON'T WORRY ABOUT ME,
I'LL BE HOME SOON.

CAP

Rain had the pickup, so that left me on foot. There was a gas station a few miles away. My plan was to go there and use the phone to call a taxi. I didn't have any money, but I still had one last check. That would get me anywhere I wanted to go.

I hadn't made this walk since the time the truck

ran out of gas. I'd forgotten how long and dusty it was. The whole way I didn't see a single vehicle. I couldn't help thinking of the crowded streets around C Average.

Finally, through the red-gold of the autumn underbrush, I could make out the Service King sign.

Maybe it was because I was upset about disobeying Rain. Whatever the reason, I didn't notice the car until I was in the middle of the road. The driver slammed on the brakes, and the tires shrieked their protest against the asphalt. The sedan spun around, its rear end swinging toward me at incredible speed. Desperately, I flung myself out of its path. The taillight missed me by inches, and I tumbled into the ditch.

The driver jumped out. "Mister, are you okay?"

I would have known that voice anywhere. *"Sophie?"*

I sat up, and there she was, peering anxiously down at me. "You maniac, where do you get off running into the middle of the road like that?"

She was right to be upset. It had been a very close call. But all I could think of was, "You got your license!"

"And they would have taken it back for running

over some *freakazoid* the very first day!"

"What are you *doing* here?" I asked, climbing out of the ditch and brushing myself off. "You're almost at Garland, you know."

"I'm taking a victory lap sixty miles from where I live. I came to find *you*, you idiot! And don't think I don't already regret it."

"*Me?*"

"That bracelet—when it came back engraved," she accused. "That wasn't from my dad, was it? *You* sent it."

I could feel my face burning bright red.

She leaned over and kissed my cheek. *Supernova* was a word I'd read in science books, but this was the first time I'd ever experienced the power of one.

"Now get in the car," she ordered. "We're going to the Halloween dance."

"What a coincidence!" As we made a U-turn and headed away from Garland, I explained my plan for the trip to C Average.

"You're crazy," she scoffed. "No taxi driver would take a check. And even if he did, how were you planning to get home?"

"I figured he'd wait until the dance was over and then—"

Her sigh cut me off. "Maybe you're better off at Camp Purple Haze. I hate to think what would happen to you in the real world."

"Well, anyway," I told her, "thanks for picking me up."

"I'm a saint," she noted. "My father said that once, but it wasn't true until right now."

As we approached the outskirts of town, there was traffic, and buildings, and lights, and people on the streets. I drank in the hustle and bustle, greeting it like an old friend. But I couldn't suppress a pang of guilt, wondering if Rain had come home and found my note.

Night had fallen by the time we reached C Average.

Sophie frowned. "Why is the building dark?"

"Power failure?" I suggested. But the nearby houses had lights on.

We turned the corner and pulled around the side of the school, stopping just short of the main driveway. There was no going in. The parking lot was jam-packed, not with cars, but with people. It would have been every bit as dark as the school, if not for hundreds and hundreds of flickering candles.

Sophie was bug-eyed. "What's going on?"

"I guess it's the Halloween dance."

"Oh, come on, even you can't think that! People dance at a dance—that's why they call it a dance! There isn't even any music!"

I had to admit it seemed pretty strange to decorate the gym and then hold the party in the parking lot.

We pulled over to the curb, and she handed me a rubber mask with a round black nose and large ears.

"What's this?" I asked.

She took a deep breath. "Costumes? Halloween? You're Mickey; I'm Minnie. Best I could do on short notice."

We put the heads on and waded into the mob. It wasn't loud, but I realized there *was* music. Somewhere in the crowd, a single boom box was playing the Beatles' *Abbey Road* album, Rain's favorite.

I surveyed the crowd through the eyeholes of my mask. "Sophie, how come we're the only ones wearing costumes?"

All at once, she put a death grip on my shoulder. "Look around—ponchos, tie-dyes, peace signs. Cap—they *are* in costume. They're dressed as *you*!"

28

NAME: **MRS. DONNELLY**

Well, of course I was worried. It was only her first full day as a licensed driver, and she'd been gone for three hours. I'd moved past the anger stage. I was no longer even miffed about being stranded at home without transportation. I was already making deals: *If Sophie comes home in one piece, I won't strangle her or even ground her. Please, please, let her be okay!*

To take my mind off the anxiety, I was cleaning out the spare room where Cap had lived for two months. I have to say he was the tidiest person in the house, as opposed to Sophie, who used the floor as a display rack for her clothing choices. I couldn't find so much as a speck of dust that had come from

Cap. As for clutter—the boy had nothing, so he couldn't possibly leave it lying around. There were a few pieces of schoolwork. One was an essay entitled: "The Most Important Invention of the Twentieth Century." What had Cap chosen to write about? The telephone? The computer? No, duct tape. In spite of my nervousness, I couldn't contain a chuckle. I remembered Garland, where duct tape had served every purpose but food.

In fact, my sweep netted only one other item—a slip of paper neatly folded in the nightstand drawer.

1 *"Effervescence" bangle, multicolor stones*
Engraving: ALL YOU NEED IS LOVE

My heart turned over in my chest. Sophie's bangle—it was from *Cap*? He had that much of a crush on her?

No, he'd pretended it was a gift from Bill. In my job, I knew that pure kindness, with no strings attached, was pretty rare. The boy was an *angel*! Whatever problems I had with Rain, I had to admit that she'd raised a truly wonderful kid.

I stared at the scrawl at the bottom of the receipt: Paid by check.

Oh, no.

I remembered the school's bank statement—the check to the jewelry store. In his innocence, Cap had purchased Sophie's bracelet with money from the Student Activity Fund!

I raced to the phone and dialed Frank Kasigi. He wasn't picking up so I tried his cell.

"What?" barked the assistant principal in a very harried tone.

"It's Flora Donnelly, Frank. I found out about the check Cap wrote to the jewelry store."

"Never mind that!" he snapped. "Meet me at the school! There's some kind of riot going on!"

I was alarmed. "Because you canceled the Halloween dance?"

"I don't think so. My custodian called me. The parking lot is full of kids with candles. They told him it's a memorial service for Cap Anderson!"

I was thunderstruck. "A *memorial service*? Cap isn't dead!"

"Well, you seem to be the only one who knows that. That's why I need you there. You're the closest thing to family he has in this town. Maybe you can convince everybody!"

"I can't get to the school," I protested. "Sophie has the car."

"Sit tight. I'll pick you up in five minutes."

My hands were shaking as I hung up the phone. Sophie AWOL, the school in turmoil, rumors Cap was dead.

What was going on here?

29

NAME: **HUGH WINKLEMAN**

In the great encyclopedia of history, if you look up *mass stupidity*, this was the picture you'd see: eleven hundred kids dressed as hippies, crammed belly to belly in a parking lot, having a candlelight memorial for someone who was probably just fine.

The idea to dress as Cap hadn't been part of Zach's original plan. Maybe it was the Halloween spirit, but the word had started spreading almost as soon as Zach and I had begun passing the flyers around the school. Picture it: the entire student body decked out in Day-Glo and beads—all except for one brain-dead pair wearing Mickey Mouse masks.

The candles had been Zach's idea. "We'll need the light," he'd told me on the way to the Dollar Store. But their effect was more than either of us could have imagined. Hundreds of tiny flames glowing orange in the dark just screamed *mourning*. Dull flickering shadows reflected off somber faces. Eerie.

Zach. I'd spent most of my life either afraid of him, jealous of him, or just hanging there while he stretched the waistband of my underwear over a parking meter. We were never going to be best friends, but I had to admire the guy. He was a genius! Not book-smart, but a master when it came to crafting his public image. Somehow, he had positioned himself as head mourner of the Anderson tragedy. Not bad, considering that a couple of days ago he was the villain of the school—him and me.

Okay, we deserved that. Setting Cap up at the pep rally was an awful thing to do, and I felt terrible about my part in it. Being angry at Cap was no excuse. I knew better than anyone what it was like to be a target for the Zachs of the world. A lot more than just my conscience was suffering. I was kicked out of the chess club for good. I had a month of

215

detentions and a black mark on my permanent record.

And how's this for ironic: the only way to avoid being branded Cap's backstabber was to get myself embroiled in yet another scheme with the same Zach Powers.

Beam me up, Scotty. There's no intelligent life on this planet.

I approached Zach. "So now what? We're not just going to stand around all night, are we?"

"Chill," he said serenely, jiggling his Dixie cup to keep his candle from going out. "We're basking in our sorrow."

I was uneasy. "I don't know. A third of these kids are positive Cap's dead, a third have him in intensive care, and the rest are just here because everyone else is. The last thing we want to do is give people too much time to think."

"Good point," Zach agreed. He hoisted himself onto the payload of the school district's flatbed truck and stopped the tape on the boom box, which was playing "Here Comes the Sun." He took the karaoke mike and flipped the switch.

"Attention, everybody! Can I have your attention up here?"

Considering the size of the crowd, we were a quiet group, gathered in clusters, speaking in hushed tones—almost like this really was a funeral. It only took a few seconds before all eyes were on Zach.

"Thanks for coming. I know if Cap could be here, he'd thank you too. Cap Anderson was our eighth grade president for just two months—two wild, fantastic months. Now he's gone, and the best way to celebrate his life is to talk about the way he touched our lives."

Then, before my amazed eyes, people began to push forward through the crowd and mount the flatbed, awaiting their turn at the microphone.

Naomi got there first. "I wasn't a nice person," she announced. "I was mean to Cap because I thought it would get me what I wanted. Then I started watching him. He showed me a whole different way to be. How to be sensitive and generous—and not just so people will say thank you, but because it's right." She drew in a tremulous breath. "I never even had a chance to tell him there's no Lorelei Lumley!"

Overcome, she gave up the mike to the seventh grader beside her. "I used to be really shy. I didn't have any friends," he confessed. "Then Cap let me work on the Halloween dance . . ."

I was blown away. One after another, these kids took center stage and poured their hearts out about how Cap had changed their lives.

"His tai chi class helped me lose eleven pounds . . ."

"I stopped picking on my little brother . . ."

"I started giving some of my paper route money to charity . . ."

"Learning about the sixties helped me get along better with my grandparents . . ."

My mind was in a whirl. The kids at C Average wouldn't share their innermost feelings if you held a machete to their throats. We lived in constant terror of letting slip some personal or embarrassing detail. We went to incredible lengths to avoid looking vulnerable or uncool.

Yet here they were, lined up to spill their guts like this was an episode of *Dr. Phil*. Because Cap had made everything A-OK.

Well, I was the number-one victim around here. And suddenly, right in front of me, was a golden opportunity to paint myself with the Cap Anderson brush that would make me A-OK too. I just had to get up there in front of the entire student body and join the fan club.

As I climbed onto the flatbed, I got my first sense of just how big this event had become. I knew the whole school was here. But now adults were starting to gather around the perimeter. The neighbors, probably. And passersby. Oh, no—it was Mr. Kasigi! I had to say my piece before our assistant principal shut the whole thing down.

I grabbed the microphone from a sixth-grade girl who insisted that tai chi had made her unbeatable at gymnastics.

"My name is Hugh Winkleman, and I was Cap's first friend at school." I experienced a brief moment of panic. I'd been so intent on getting the floor that I hadn't given a thought to what I should say. Eleven hundred faces peered earnestly up at me. This was no time to be timid. If I was going to do this, I had to let it all hang out.

I bit down hard on the side of my mouth until I felt two giant tears well out of my eyes and roll down my cheeks.

"Cap Anderson was the greatest person it's ever been my honor to know. How are we ever going to get along without our president?"

I could see Mr. Kasigi pushing through the crowd. It was time to give this a big finish. This was my shining hour. Hugh Winkleman would be the school joke no longer!

I dropped the mike to the flatbed, raised both arms to the heavens, and howled, *"Cap! You were too young to die!"*

I could hear sobs breaking out all around me. And then a muffled but strangely familiar voice called, "Hugh—don't cry!"

I goggled. One of the kids in Mickey Mouse masks waded through the crush to reach the truck. He stopped just below me and pulled off the mouse head.

"See?" announced Cap Anderson. "Everything's okay! I'm not dead!"

30

NAME: **ZACH POWERS**

Wow.

What a lightning strike. Like crashing your own funeral.

Hugh fell off the flatbed. I didn't blame him. I was seriously thinking about taking a dive myself. This didn't make me look so great either.

The people close in realized who had just shown up. They went berserk, hugging Cap and shrieking with joy. Farther back, there was a buzz of confusion. Something was going on, but nobody could figure out what.

Finally, a couple of guys in the front row helped Cap onto the truck. The wind took his long blond hair and blew it into a halo around his face, backlit by a streetlamp.

The roar from eleven hundred throats combined shock, disbelief, happiness, and even love. I was used to crowd noise from playing football, but I never experienced anything like this. The ground shook. The echoes bounced off houses and buildings. It was unreal.

The hairball tried to say something. Forget it. There was no way anyone was going to hear him over the sounds of celebration that he was still among us. He had a couple of shiners and a cut on his nose where Darryl had decked him. Yet it was obvious to everybody that the eighth grade president was not hospitalized, not suffering from amnesia, not in a vegetative state, and was very, very much alive.

Naomi, her face glowing and streaked with tears, reached down for the fallen microphone and handed it to Cap. Still the thunderous ovation went on. I clocked six full minutes, but it might have been longer.

Finally, the tumult died away, and an expectant silence covered the crowd.

Cap shuffled uncomfortably and said, "This

isn't the Halloween dance . . . is it?"

A wave of laughter greeted this. I'll bet I was the only one out of the eleven hundred who knew that he wasn't joking—me and Winkleman.

"I can't believe so many people were worried about me," he went on. "I'm fine. I just had to go home because Rain got out of the hospital. My life isn't here anymore. I live at Garland Farm."

He seemed to spot someone at the edge of the crowd and gave a shy wave in that direction. I followed his line of vision and noticed an older lady who waved back with a cane. Even if she hadn't made that gesture, I would have been able to pick her out. She was the only adult in hippie clothes—peasant blouse, long cotton skirt, Day-Glo headband with a yin/yang disk in the center of her forehead. Stunned disbelief was the only way to describe her reaction to the sight of Cap on the receiving end of all that love. Trust me, I could relate.

"Rain," he said gravely, "I'm sorry I came here when you said not to. I only did it because I really wanted to see a dance. But there was another reason too. I left school before I had a chance to say goodbye to everybody. So I guess I should start that now."

He turned to the right side of the front row. "Good-bye Jason . . . good-bye Trudy . . . good-bye Leo . . . good-bye Ariel . . . good-bye Trevor . . . good-bye Mike . . ."

There was a titter of amusement that died out quickly when people realized that he wasn't stopping.

". . . Good-bye Daniel . . . good-bye Raj . . . good-bye Heather . . . good-bye Naomi . . . good-bye Jordan . . . good-bye Lena . . . good-bye Hugh . . ."

This was getting weird. He went all the way across the first row, and then started along the second in the opposite direction. By this time, there was absolute silence in the parking lot.

". . . Good-bye Daisy . . . good-bye Emily . . . good-bye Julius . . . good-bye Sam . . ."

He was halfway down the third row when I finally clued in. Cap wasn't planning to say, "Good-bye, everybody." He was saying good-bye—to *everybody*!

I had a flashback to the assembly two months ago, when Kasigi had first proclaimed him president. As a goof, I'd told the kid that he had to learn everyone's name. And somehow, by some *miracle*, he'd actually done it!

". . . Good-bye Severin . . . good-bye Jay . . .

good-bye Kelly . . . good-bye Phil . . ."

No football player could fail to recognize what I was experiencing right then. It was the moment on the field when you realize that you're completely, hopelessly outclassed. When I looked at the hairball on the payload, I didn't see the eighth grade president; I saw the Super Bowl champions. There was no defeating a kid who could memorize an entire school.

". . . Good-bye Natasha . . . good-bye Annabel . . . good-bye Patrick . . . good-bye Marco . . ."

It took almost an hour. Nobody moved. We barely uttered a sound. It was the kind of performance that came along once in a lifetime, and you didn't want to miss one second. It was like being a part of history.

Eleven hundred students. Eleven hundred names. He never hesitated, and he never got one wrong.

We wouldn't even have known he was finished except that he set the microphone down on the flatbed and started to climb off.

Nobody let him. Darryl rushed over, hoisted him onto his shoulders, and began to tote him through the cheering crowd. Naomi and Lena were at their side, screaming their heads off. I waded over to join them. After all, they were my friends, and it was time to bury the hatchet. Hippie-loving friends were better than no friends at all.

Cap called down to us, "Rain's waiting," so we headed for the older lady in the yin/yang headband.

It was slow going, because everybody in the place wanted to high-five the living legend. Navigating all those outstretched arms was like plowing through a field of bamboo.

When Darryl finally deposited Cap onto the tarmac beside Rain, she barely noticed him. She was being chewed out by a younger woman who I'd seen around the school a few times.

". . . What he did with those checks—as an adult, he could go to jail for that!"

Rain's face was ashen. "He tried to give the school's money to charity?"

"Who taught him any different?" the woman ranted. "I remember your brand of education! None of us had the faintest idea how to survive in the real world! I was lucky—I had parents. Who's Cap going to turn to? You won't live forever, you know. . . ."

So that was what happened with the checks! It

wasn't Kasigi; it was pure Cap, taking the hippie thing too far, as usual. And instead of getting arrested for it—which would have happened to the rest of us—he was elevated to rock-star status.

Cap regarded his grandmother nervously. "There was supposed to be a dance. I'm not sure what happened. Are you mad at me?"

"Of course not," she told him. Then she turned to the younger woman. "Good-bye, Floramundi." It didn't sound friendly.

"Bye, Cap!" piped up Darryl as grandmother and grandson got into a double-parked pickup truck.

"We love you!" Naomi yelled as the two sets of hippie hair disappeared down the street.

The woman called Floramundi hugged a really good-looking high school girl who was holding a rubber Minnie Mouse mask. I did a double take. *She* was Cap's *date*? The Minnie to his Mickey?

Unbelievable! While he was busy turning C Average on its ear, Cap still had time to pick up a supermodel. Had the whole world gone crazy? I spun around like a victim of amnesia, desperately searching the parking lot for a glimpse of something—*anything*—that made sense.

And there, in the dispersing crowd, my eyes found Hugh Winkleman. He looked terrible—his clothes disheveled, his glasses bent and askew. He was such a dweeb, but he was almost *my* dweeb now—the only kid who'd stuck by me while the whole school flocked to the hairball.

I was kind of starting to appreciate that guy.

31

NAME: **CAPRICORN ANDERSON**

I was driving the pickup on the dirt lane alongside our orchard when I got arrested again.

I was surprised when the siren blurped and the lights started flashing. Rain had told me to stay off the county roads, but that I'd be okay so long as I stuck to Garland property.

When I said that to the officer, though, his answer shocked me: "This isn't Garland anymore. The land belongs to Skyline Realty and Development. And you're driving without a license."

With that, he loaded me into the back of his squad car.

The county sheriff's office was a lot smaller than

the police station they'd taken me to after I drove Mr. Rodrigo to the hospital in the school bus. It had only one room, and there wasn't even a lockup—just a metal ring they could handcuff people to.

They didn't do that to me. They just sat me in a chair and told me to wait while they made phone calls.

I stared out the window, feeling pretty low. Rain was going to be mad when she found out about Skyline Realty and Development. Dealing with big companies was one of the things she'd formed Garland to get away from. Who knew what a hassle it was going to be to straighten out this mistake?

She'd been so busy lately—away a lot, and really quiet when she was home, listening to her favorite songs from the sixties on our record player. "The Times They Are A-Changin'" by Bob Dylan especially seemed to fascinate her. She let it repeat over and over again.

"Bob Dylan was right," I'd said one night.

She looked sad. "I used to think change was a *choice*. That you could avoid it if you stuck with your convictions. Now—" She shook her head. "I just don't know."

I'd almost asked her if she'd heard that they hardly ever made vinyl records anymore—that it was all CDs and MP3s and DAT files. I decided not to. Even more change was probably the last thing she wanted to deal with.

It had been a tough couple of weeks since the Halloween dance that wasn't a dance at all. I wondered if I'd ever be happy again. I knew I didn't fit in at C Average, but Garland wasn't exactly right for me either.

Knowing eleven hundred people can spoil you for being alone.

I didn't regret my time in real school. I learned a lot—like when you have a checking account, your money is separate from all the other money in the bank. And when you write a check, the number you put in the little box gets subtracted from what you have.

I learned that you can't fix a china figurine with duct tape because it doesn't look right. And I learned a new vocabulary word: klutz.

I learned about lockers and reruns and Giga-Volumizer. I almost learned about dances, but I didn't.

The most important thing I learned is how many

things out there I still needed to learn about. I wanted to, but it didn't seem like I was going to get the chance.

On the other side of the window, the sunlit world had never appeared so wide and tempting.

A very fancy car with a shiny new paint job screeched up to the curb. I recognized the hood ornament that looked sort of like a peace sign. I knew from *Trigonometry and Tears* that it was called a Mercedes, and it cost a lot of money. I was puzzled to notice a yellowed bumper sticker on the back—*War Is Not Healthy for Children and Other Living Things*. The only place I'd ever seen one like it was on our old pickup truck.

A blond, stylishly dressed woman slipped from behind the wheel, talking on her cell phone. With her free hand, she reached back into the car and pulled out a cane.

Rain's cane!

I did a double take. The hair was different, the clothes were different, and I'd never seen the car. But this was Rain!

She came in and gave me a hug. I felt the familiar contours of her love beads through the fabric of her designer blouse.

She announced, "Not bad for an old grandma, right?"

"Rain, what happened? You've—*changed*!"

She took a deep breath. "Brace yourself, Capricorn. I've got a lot to tell you."

"I've got a lot to tell *you*," I interrupted. "I got arrested again. And the police say some development company owns Garland! What are we going to do?"

"Some development company *does* own Garland. I should know. I sold it to them."

I was horrified. "*Sold?* You always said no one owns the earth, so no one can buy it or sell it!"

She was patient. "That wasn't me, Cap. I was quoting the ancient Hopi Indians. Forty years ago, when Garland began, I purchased the land with money I borrowed from my parents. We lived as a true commune, sharing everything, and I was a partner—nothing more, nothing less. But the deed was always in my name, so it was always mine to sell." She waved her hand to quell my protest. "Calm down. I wouldn't let them build some gated fortress of McMansions for the masters of the universe. There's going to be affordable housing for all income levels. And a park with a flower garden.

I thought that was a nice touch."

I was distraught. This went against everything I'd been taught to believe in. She was taking the entire Garland value system and junking it! I understood that she had the *legal* right to sell it; what I didn't understand was—

"*Why?*" I demanded. "You lived this way for forty years! You kept on long after all the other communities and communes shut down and disappeared! Why stop now?"

"Oh, Cap, I thought you knew. I did it for you."

"*Me?*"

"My accident was a wake-up call. I'm not planning on dying anytime soon, but you'll eventually outlive me. When I'm gone, you'll have to get along in the real world. That just won't happen if we stay at Garland. It would be criminal for me to let you face life with no more street smarts than a newborn baby. Although," she added meaningfully, "nobody could say that your first try wasn't a success. How many people get to attend their own memorial service—along with eleven hundred of their closest friends?"

It was as if my entire universe had been twisted inside out. Was this Rain, or some stranger who had

taken control of her body? Yet, in a way, I was seeing my grandmother more clearly than ever before.
I was the one who had been born and raised at
Garland; Rain grew up in San Francisco. I may have
been completely helpless in the outside world, but
she wasn't.

"Besides," she went on, her eyes twinkling,
"some incredible things have been happening in the
real estate market since the sixties. I just sold
Garland for seventeen million dollars."

I stared at her for a long time. "That's a lot, isn't
it?"

She nodded. "We're rich. But don't worry. We're
not turning our backs on what Garland represents.
With this money, we can accomplish more than we
could by living there for a thousand years. You had
the right idea with those Student Activity Fund
checks. I see a charitable foundation—the Garland
Foundation, maybe. The sixties may be over, but
the spirit is stronger than ever."

I chewed on this. "So what happens now? Where
are we going to live?"

"I bought us a condo," she replied. "It won't be
ready for a few days, and I'll be tied up with the
details. So I've arranged for you to stay with a

family near the new school you'll be attending."

I must have looked miserable, because she added, "You'll like these people. Honestly." She took the cell phone from her suit pocket, flipped it open, and handed it to me.

"Uh—hello?"

A voice said, "Hey, freakazoid, I hear you're moving back in."

The grin must have split my face. "So the new school is—"

Rain smiled too. "I can think of eleven hundred kids who are going to be really happy to have you back."

And I already knew all their names.

G☮RDON KORMAN

is the author of more than fifty popular young adult and middle-grade novels, including *Born to Rock*, *Son of the Mob*, and the best-selling *Island*, *Kidnapped*, and *Macdonald Hall* series.

Born in Montreal and raised in Toronto, Gordon lives with his family in New York.